BUCK is an original publication of Avon Books. This work has never before appeared in book form.

AVON BOOKS
A division of
The Hearst Corporation
105 Madison Avenue
New York, New York 10016

Copyright © 1986 by Tamela Larimer
Published by arrangement with the author
Library of Congress Catalog Card Number: 86-90774
ISBN: 0-380-75172-0
RL: 5.6

First Avon Flare Printing: November 1986

AVON BOOKS TRADEMARK REG. U.S. PAT. OFF. AND IN OTHER COUNTRIES, MARCA REGISTRADA, HECHO EN CANADA

Printed in Canada

UNV 10 9 8 7 6 5 4

Dear Reader:

In 1984, we created the Avon Flare Young Adult Novel Competition to give young writers the opportunity of having their work judged by a major publisher. At the same time, we at Avon are always searching for new talent and are delighted when we find it, waiting to be discovered, among our own readers.

Four hundred of you responded to our competition. Each entry was read and carefully considered by our editorial staff. You moved us, entertained us, and impressed us, not only with your talent but with the diversity of your concerns and the depth of your perceptions of the world in which you live.

We are pleased and proud to publish the winning entry in this year's contest. Tamela Larimer's brilliant imagination has created BUCK, the kind of larger-than-life figure you always hope you'll meet one day. And she tells Buck's story in the voice of Rich Candy, who could be you or your best friend. We hope you'll enjoy reading this moving story by one of your fellow readers.

Ellen E. Krieger
Editorial Director
Avon Books for Young Readers

BUCK

TAMELA LARIMER

AN AVON FLARE BOOK

To everyone who told me it would happen

Chapter 1

I first met Buck in my—the family's—blue sports car.

It was the beginning of August. You know how it is at the beginning of August. That's when everybody gets his first whiff of the end of summer. Back-to-school ads crop up thicker than goldenrod. The last-chance-for-summer-romance rush starts. Grass dries brown and crackly. Your shoes stick to the road. Dogs sleep on and under porches. Band camp starts. School notices and calendars and schedules pile up on the dining-room table. Nostalgic thoughts of summer and eager thoughts of the new school year set in at the same time, and you drink Pepsi or whatever and wonder if you're really ready to go back. Suntanning gets really intensive. Crickets make noise all night long.

This kind of thing is especially sharp for a senior-to-be like me. It's your last year in the old system and you know it. Next year you'll either be slaving away at some job or slaving away at some college, so you've got to make the very best out of what time you have left.

Don't get me wrong. Nobody sits around brooding about this stuff. It just makes itself known in a kind of excited uncertainty that's covered up quicker than thought by plans of college and careers and clothes and rumors of who is seeing whom and who broke up with whom over vacation. You concentrate on having as much fun as you can without getting into trouble.

To get back to the point. It was the beginning of August. Happy month.

And here I was, Rich Candy, your average middle-class suburban-type guy, walking back to the car with my Foodland paycheck stuck in my front pocket and a Thrift drugstore bag in my hand filled with a birthday card for my Aunt Carrie that my mother had asked me to get and a couple of rolls of peppermint Lifesavers for myself. I'm addicted to peppermint Lifesavers.

I had come up on the wrong side of the row, so I squeezed between one of those mural-painted vans and a dented old Plymouth to get to my car.

And there was someone in my car.

God, was I mad.

I was so mad that for a few seconds I couldn't see, and sure as anything, I didn't think.

I barreled up there and threw open the driver's-side door—the door with the window I'd left half open.

This kid—I could see now that it was just a kid, a guy around my own age—jumped so high he hit his head on the roof. It's a miracle he didn't knock himself out, considering the impact of metal on his skull. I really startled him.

He leapt for the passenger door and threw himself hard against it. But the car in the next space had pulled too close. The door opened about four inches and then scraped into the other car. And for some reason that made me madder than anything, this jerk scraping the paint like that.

Head thrown back, muscles tense, this kid plastered himself against the partly open door and stared out the windshield with these wide eyes. One hand clawed on the dashboard, and the other dug into the headrest. He looked like an animal, an animal trapped and frozen beyond panic.

Something about the way he cringed made me stop a minute. All the mad in me drained out onto the pavement right around my Nikes, and I wondered what could make somebody break into a car like that. There'd have to be something wrong, really hurting wrong, to come down to doing something like that. So here I was looking at this tensed-up kid with absolutely no idea what I should do. I stood there for a minute, maybe, though it seemed a lot longer. Finally, I came up with something—something really stupid. I said, "You know you're in my car?"

The kid kind of jumped again, shoulders hunching. He kept his face turned to look out across the lot, but his eyes moved to catch mine.

They were golden brown eyes, opaque animal eyes that didn't reveal anything going on inside. They were glittery eyes—set above high, slanted cheekbones on a tan, strongly angled face—wary and hooded beneath wisps of hair the color of a wheat field at sunrise. I'd never seen eyes like his, color or expression, on anyone else.

He said to me, "You a genius or what?"

My mouth tightened. I could feel my blood rush. I kept hanging in the door of my car, not getting in but not staying out. A little bit of anger had seeped back in. "What're you doing in my car?"

3

"Finding myself some food." He wasn't being smart, wasn't being cocky. He just answered.

"Food? God—" I swore and slapped the drugstore bag onto the seat beside him. "Lifesavers," I said shortly, pointing.

I thought he was going to jump again, but after flicking his glance from me to the bag and back to me again, he relaxed. The cords in his neck and shoulders loosened, and his face wasn't so taut. He reached for the bag. "Thanks." He took a roll and snapped it in half and then ate one after another, barely chewing. I think he swallowed a couple of them whole.

When he was done, which was in about forty-five seconds, he said, real lightly and not looking at me. "You planning to take me in or what?"

That got me. "Huh?"

He smiled a little. "If you're not taking me in, how about letting me out."

I was back on guard now. I was watching him. "Just wait a minute," I said. "What were you doing in my car?"

"I told you. Finding food."

A laugh caught in my throat. "Eat cars often?" I was being really sarcastic—my natural reaction with a jerk like that in my car.

He pointed to the tape deck, my almost brandnew tape deck. "That piece of car is money. Money's food and maybe a place to stay."

"Place to—" My ears pricked. "Where do you live, anyway?"

"Last mailing address was L.A."

I absorbed that without a fight. I think I expected something like it. "Mmm, L.A.," I said. I gripped the steering wheel for support. Outer Pittsburgh is a really great place, low-key and with-it at the same time, but it's not too glamorous. "Listen, I know a car in the middle of a

4

miracle mile in the middle of Pittsburgh is a great place to visit and all, but what in the—"

He cut me off. "I had to go somewhere," he said sharply. There was a strange desperation in his voice I'd never heard in anyone's voice before. It had a laid-bare quality to it. It was something you could almost pity. "Somewhere," he repeated a lot more softly. "Only so much money, and once my ...mother, well, said she was from here...." He trailed off and looked at me, eyes blank and golden brown.

I was starting to feel extremely uncomfortable. "Where is your mother?"

He smiled again. He was a toothpaste commercial come to life when he smiled, and it was cold contrast to the hardness in his expression as he said, "Six feet under."

It stung me that he could say that so matter-of-factly, so calmly. It wasn't normal. "Shut the door," I ordered.

This time he was the one who was startled. "Huh?"

"Shut the door!"

He did it without another word.

I jammed the key into the ignition and pulled out of the parking space a lot faster than I should've. I almost knocked off someone's bumper, but I didn't care. I was hot and angry and confused. When I got out onto the main road, I didn't spare the gas, and it took another five minutes before I realized I was biting my lip.

I shot a glance at my passenger. He slouched in the seat easy and at home, arms crossed, chin on his chest. And sure enough, just like before, the anger was diluted, drained right out of me. Why, I don't know. Maybe because he didn't put up any defense—at least, not any I could recognize—and I felt guilty for wanting to kill him,

5

even if I did have a perfectly good reason. Maybe that's it. I just don't know.

"Why'd you say that?" I asked him finally.

"What?"

"About your mother."

"Because it's true. Something wrong with the truth?"

I didn't answer that. "You have anybody ... anywhere?"

"On my own."

"You staying anywhere?"

"Nowhere in particular."

"What about money?"

"Spent my last dollar day before yesterday."

"You know there's places you could go ... I could drive you—"

"I won't go to them." There was no compromise in those words.

I didn't waste my breath arguing. Let him do as he pleased. "Fine. None of my business if you want to be stupid."

"Let me off."

"Huh—?"

"Let me off." He slumped against the door and stared down at the road spinning under the tires. He looked miserable.

I couldn't do that. Anger was gone, and pity had taken its place again. I couldn't just dump him on the highway. Thinking fast, I said, "Eat with me first. . . . Kind of make up for the meal you didn't get from my deck," I couldn't help adding wryly.

He flashed me this straight easy grin, and now those golden brown eyes reflected something. They were warm like a dog's, warm and glowing, but the glow had an edge.

* * *

We ended up eating at McDonald's, and I blew six bucks feeding this kid. Not that I minded. I had an uncashed check in my pocket to keep me going. But it was unbelievable the way he wolfed those Big Macs. I had bought a Coke for myself, and I swear he'd eaten three Macs before I was halfway through. I'd never seen anyone eat the way this kid was eating. Maybe because I'd never met anyone that hungry before.

I mean, you see the pictures of starving children in Third World countries, but unless you've truly been hungry, you just can't understand.

So I sat there in the plastic booth shaking the ice around in my cup, waiting for him to finish. It was a short wait. He mashed together all the cartons and napkins and junk and reached around to throw it into the garbage receptacle we were sitting next to. Then he leaned back and closed his eyes and looked like he was going to fall asleep.

I stared. "You're welcome," I said finally. I toyed with an ashtray and dropped it on purpose to wake him up.

"Thanks," he mumbled, not even opening his eyes. "Name's Buck."

"Rich," I said back. "Rich Candy."

His eyes opened. There they were, golden brown and curious. "What?"

"Rich Candy. That's my name. Capital R-i-c-h. Capital C-a-n-d-y." I always spell out my name like that when I get a reaction at introductions. It's a device for making people feel guilty for asking about it.

He seemed to take that in and chew on it and then file it away in the back of his mind. He leaned across the table. "Where do I go from here?" he asked. His face was drawn up tight, and he sat on the edge of his seat, perched to run.

I made a decision then. It was one of those cas-

7

ual decisions you don't realize will change your whole life until it's too late. It was nothing big then, just some self-important charity work on my part. I couldn't just say, Hey, good luck, see you later, and leave him. That would be pretty low on my part, when the guy obviously had problems. I figured I'd take this stray home with me, hand him over to Dad, and let him take care of it.

So I said, "Come on," and went to the doors.

Hesitation was all over him. It was push and pull all the way. I knew he was thinking exactly what I would've been thinking in his place: that he couldn't trust anybody, especially not anybody who'd caught him trying to steal his tape deck; at the same time, he had no other choice. Finally, me standing there with one foot out of the door, he pushed himself up and followed me without a word.

He'd made a choice, and I'd made a decision.

The two of them together started a whole chain reaction.

On the way home we talked—or at first I talked, rambling on and on about nothing much, and after a while Buck opened up. Or maybe he quit holding up the walls is a better way to say it.

He told me things. Most of it I could hardly believe. I didn't want to believe.

But he didn't lie. You can tell when somebody's lying.

He gave me his autobiography. It was sad. Especially because to him it was all normal.

He'd lived in L.A. for as long as he could remember, but he'd moved around the city a lot. He'd lived with his mother, but he didn't say much about her. All I could figure was that she was drunk a big part of the time and that she had trouble handling her money. Buck told me he used

8

to have to hide the welfare check to keep her from spending it all on booze. Oh, and she had a constant string of male friends—paying male friends. I think Buck hated them, all of them, and I don't blame him.

It sounded to me like Buck had had one heck of a job baby-sitting his mother.

He went to school out there, and he used to push for extra money. He never got caught, and he never used anything himself. "Sometimes I wanted to," he said. "But I'm not stupid. I didn't have the money." He used what money he got for living, pure basic living.

He asked me if I'd ever done anything. I told him no, which was the truth. He just nodded and said, "Good for you." He was sincere about it.

I was dumb enough to ask about a father. His head jerked back, and his eyes fastened on the side-view mirror. "Your guess is as good as mine." He pulled silence around him like a blanket after that.

I'd been driving like a cabbie, taking all the long ways around and taking turns that headed away from home rather than toward it, all because I wanted to hear this story. But when he shut his mouth, I should've taken the hint. I should've kept my own mouth shut. If I had, there wouldn't have been any reason for us to have to trust each other. But no, I just had to know more.

I asked, "What about your mother ... what happened?" I tried not to push it, but I think he could tell how bad I was itching to know.

He hesitated, staring down at his hands as he flexed his fingers. After a minute, though, he said slowly, "She died right before I turned sixteen. They said it was a heart attack. I don't know anything except that it happened one night I was gone and that it was the best thing that ever happened to her and the worst thing that ever happened to me. I was going to quit school and get myself a job or something and mind my own business in the place we had. But that wasn't what the authorities had in mind. They wanted to shuffle me off to some home...."

"What was wrong with that?"

"I didn't want to. They were going to... tie me up."

I understood. As bad as he'd had it, he'd always been free to do as he pleased. He ran himself, and he ran a household—if you want to call it that—and he did it just fine. He was happy with it. He was used to being his own boss. His freedom was all he had, and he didn't want to lose it no matter what.

"So what'd you do?" I said, tapping the brake around a tight curve.

"The only thing I could. I ran out before they could get me. I only had seventy-two dollars...." He trailed off again. He'd done that a lot while he was telling me all that stuff about himself and his mother, kind of looking ahead and into himself at the same time.

"So what'd you do?" I repeated, prodding.

I wish I'd shut my mouth.

He shrugged. "As much as I could with only seventy-two dollars. I got in touch with the guy I used to sell stuff for, and he got me in touch with a guy who had these sleazy little rooms you could rent for forty a month if you worked for him.... What I got was dirt, but I just couldn't do any better, Candy...."

It was the first time he'd said my name, first or last, and he said it in a weirdly apologetic way. I should've known then it was really high time to shut my mouth. It's like once you give the lamb you're fattening up for Easter dinner a name,

10

there's no way you can kill it. Once he used my name, a bond started to grow between us. I could've killed it right then, but I was stupid and I didn't see it.

"Why'd you leave the place?" I wanted to know. "If you had a job and a place—"

He laughed then. It was a bitter, hollow laugh. It was a laugh that tingled the skin on the back of my neck and turned my guts cold. "You want to know what my job was?" He laughed again, that same ugly, self-corroding laugh. "My job was to sell myself to whoever came knocking at the door."

I knew what he meant, but it didn't register right away because I didn't want it to. I didn't want to know any more. But not wanting to know didn't do a thing. It was too late. I felt sick.

His voice was tight and hoarse. "I don't know why I told you that," he said—so fast I could barely understand him. "I never told anyone that. Never. I don't know why I told you that." He was talking in sobs now. I didn't know how to handle something like this. I couldn't shy away from it because he was right there beside me and because ... the bond was already there. I felt for him. That's the only way I can put it. I felt for him, and all that pent-up pain was pouring onto me.

I didn't need it.

I didn't want it.

But it was there.

"I don't know why I told you that," he said again, choking on his words. "I never told anyone. Oh, God. Listen to me, Rich. Listen to me. I had to do it. I had to. I didn't have a choice. I hated myself. I felt like dirt, and I still do. I never told anyone this. . . . Listen, Rich. Kill yourself before you give yourself away, because you're all you got. They take pride away from you, and you never get it

11

back. I don't know why I'm telling you this.... Man, I don't know, I just don't know.... Never give up anything of yourself if you don't get the same in return.... That's why I ran, 'cause I had to. I couldn't stand myself...."

My eyes blurred. The road was gray and unfocused in front of me. He'd dropped the shield, and now I was the only one to hold him up after he did it. There was that bond between us, strong and heavy and forever. It was a bond of secrets and of knowing and understanding. He needed that bond, and I didn't say no to it. I couldn't say no to it. I wouldn't have wanted someone to say no to me.

That's how I first met Buck.

Chapter 2

By the time I pulled in the driveway, everything was back to normal, normal as it could be, at least on the surface. Buck had covered up quickly, almost too quickly, and I used a version of the hear-it-and-forget trick—you know, blocking it out—to keep myself in control.

But one thing was different. There was that bond between us now, and there was no ignoring it.

He was really reluctant to go into the house, probably because he didn't know what to expect and was just a little nervous, even though it didn't show and he wouldn't admit it. I ended up convincing him by telling him that no one was home except my little sister Christy, which was true. Everyone else was out.

So he came in the house. Now, the house I live in isn't too bad, but it's not that amazing, either. It's an average white with brown trim two-story in the middle of an average clipped lawn with hedges and one maple tree in the front. Inside is some average nice furniture and a TV and a microwave and a whole bunch of other regular household stuff. But he kept looking all around, and right off he said, "I'd give a lot to live in a place like this." It wasn't like he was awed or anything—he wasn't from the jungles of Africa—but he was quiet, and I could tell he felt out of place. Pretty soon, though, the strangeness wore off and he made himself at home. That was a way he had, being able to adjust so fast and easy like that.

I took him into the kitchen—kind of thinking in the back of my mind how that was the best place because there wasn't anything of a whole lot of value in there—and checked for notes on the refrigerator and asked him if he wanted something just as if he were any old buddy from school. He said no, telling me all those Big Macs would keep him a half-hour or so. I laughed, a little surprised at the easy answer.

That's when Christy bounced into the kitchen from the back yard. Christy's eleven, right between Barbies and boys, and she's got blond hair and a pug nose and bright blue eyes. She'll be beautiful when she's older. Anyway, Christy came in from the backyard all grubby from digging around in the flowers, and her friend Missy from up the street trailed behind her, along with Captain, our German shepherd.

"We want Popsicles," she announced to me.

"Good for you," I told her. "Go for it."

"Jerk," she said lovingly, flouncing over to the freezer. "Just for that, I won't get you one."

"I don't want one."

"Well, maybe *he* does." She handed Missy an orange and took a purple for herself.

I decided to go along with her. I raised an eye-

14

brow and, carefully serious, said, "Well, Buck. She could be right. *Do* you want one?"

He kept up the seriousness. "It's all up to the lady," he said, shrugging and holding out his hands.

Christy just loved that. "He knows one when he sees one," she said, so prim and regal I almost laughed in her face. She found another purple and gave it to him. "That's purple," she said. "The best one. It's my favorite." And then she sprang away, purple drips running down her hand, and slipped through the screen door, Missy dribbling orange behind her.

Buck thoughtfully peeled the paper from his sticky purple Popsicle and bit off the top and chewed it.

I cringed. Just the thought of something that cold on my teeth made my head ache.

He chewed his slow way through the whole thing without saving a word. I didn't mind the silence at all. It was comfortable, not empty or stiff. We were there, and there was nothing that needed to be said at the moment, so we were quiet.

He bent the wooden stick between two fingers until it cracked and splintered. Then he looked at me. "Sometimes I used to think it would be great to have a little sister or brother," he said. "Someone to talk to...look out for...y'know? But every time I thought about it, I'd see what happened to kids where I came from...and I didn't want it anymore."

I looked down at the table. I didn't know what to say. "Well, she's a good kid," I said finally. "Talk to her sometime."

I left the Thrift bag with Aunt Carrie's card on the kitchen counter and took Buck and the last roll of peppermint Lifesavers upstairs to my room.

I leapt up the steps two at a time out of habit, waiting on the landing for Buck to catch up and rambling at the mouth the whole time. "I used to have to share my room with my brother," I told him. "Thank God I have it to myself now. He's completely unreal.... Look at this." We were on the second floor now, and I nudged at the door to Bill's room with my foot. It swung open about halfway and then ground into something, but it was enough to see most of the lair he'd created for himself from the old guest room. All kinds of weird posters plastered every available inch of the wall and ceiling. The blinds were down, and he'd left his black-violet lamp on as always, and the effect was really eerie. "See that weight set?" I said, gesturing at a shadowy corner. "That's mine, for crying out loud. He has everything else he could want—I mean, look at that stereo system—but he's gotta have my weights too." Just thinking about it got me kind of disgusted, so I slammed the door shut again, almost bashing in Buck's face—he'd been just looking and looking, like he couldn't believe it was really all there.

"He thinks he's the greatest thing that ever hit the sophomore class," I said, pulling Buck on down the hall, not paying any attention to the fact that his mind was still on everything he'd seen in Bill's room. "He's got some severe symptoms of mirror-love, you know? He spent the whole summer frying himself and putting stuff in his hair to make it blond.... And he lifts with *my* weights. Gotta make those fifteen-year-old biceps bulge...."

Quietly Buck said, "You live good here."

That got me for a minute. I held my breath, reflecting. "I guess," I said finally.

We went into my room. I flipped on my box, which is what I used for a stereo—because really that's what it was, a miniature stereo—and I

16

stretched out on my bed. Buck made himself comfortable on the floor, laying himself out with his chin on his arms.

The window was open, and I could see out onto the street. It was shimmering hot and sunny, and Edna across the street was watering her lawn, and some junior-high kids had a game of football going. Really, it was too good a day to be in the house, especially on my day off, but I wasn't thinking about that. I was thinking about what to do about Buck.

We sat there and listened to WDVE and talked. Once I heard Christy roaming around downstairs, but other than that, the house was silent. Summer sounds were distant and droning, and I didn't even consciously hear them. A lawn mower's buzz is the essence of summer in the suburbs.

"Well," I started after a drifting kind of silence, "what do you want to do?"

"Do?" he echoed. "I'll do what I always do."

"What's that?"

"Go somewhere."

"But you don't have anywhere to go."

His laugh was short and wry. "Never stopped me before."

"If you could do anything you wanted right now with no problem, what would you do?"

"It won't happen, so I'm not going to torture myself thinking about it. Okay?"

I wasn't making much progress. "C'mon," I said. "Just think about it. What would you do if you could do anything you wanted?"

He chewed contemplatively on his thumb. "Get a hotel room. I guess."

A hotel room? I shook my head a little. Was that as far ahead as he could think? Then what?

"I'll find something." He was matter-of-fact, calm.

That calm made me nervous because I knew, sure as anything, if I were alone and faced against life like he was, I'd be scared out of my mind. Then again, he didn't know any better. He didn't know he was supposed to be scared. I said, "What if you could stay here tonight...what would you do?"

I don't know what I thought he'd say. All I know is that the last thing I expected was what he did say. "Thanks. I'll do it."

Startled, I said, "Huh?"

He looked at me. "You were offering me a place for the night, weren't you?"

Commercials blared on the station. "Well..." I considered it, really considered it. "Yeah. I guess. Why not? Wouldn't hurt anything."

"You won't report me?"

"Hey...don't worry about it. I understand. I'd have done the same thing. You needed that deck...." I felt good saying that, good like a generous old millionaire helping the widow with the month's rent.

"No...that's not what I meant," he said, deflating my bubble a little. "I mean, you won't tell your, ah, parents about me....You got parents, right?"

"Yeah. But I can't hide you in a closet, y'know? They're going to ask about you."

"Don't tell them anything."

I raised an eyebrow. He didn't know my parents—or any real parents, probably, for that matter—if he thought something like that would work. "It won't work," I told him. "They know when you're not telling them something."

"Tell them...I'm a friend or something. I don't care. Just don't report me. I won't stay if you report me."

His conditions put my back up a little. "What

18

are you so tight about?" I said, annoyance under-lining the words. "I'm trying to do you a favor."

Golden brown eyes pinned to my own. "They'll turn me in somewhere."

"Oh, c'mon. They're not the police. They'll understand, believe me. You just needed money. . . ."

His mouth tightened. "I'm not talking about the thing with the car," he said. "What I'm saying is that they'll try to turn me in to some home."

"I don't think they would."

"Sure they would." He shrugged. "They won't kick me out on the street. They won't want me to stay around, either. They'll turn me in some-where, and if they try—"

I finished for him. "You'll run."

He nodded.

"So it comes down to running, no matter what."

His eyes lowered, and he caught his lip in his teeth. Voice so low I hardly heard, he said, "It would be nice to have a breather, though."

"C'mon. Stay. It's just for a night." He looked so down right then that a rock would've felt sorry for him. "C'mon. Breathe a little."

"You won't—"

"I won't report you. Okay? I promise. Why would I report you?"

"Thanks," he said softly.

Things never happen the way you think they'll happen.

My mom's car pool dropped her off at the door at five-fifteen. I went downstairs to talk to her and took a foot-dragging Buck with me. He might have wanted to believe the situation didn't faze him, but he was cracking his knuckles, uneasy, and it showed.

I found Mom in the den kicking off her high-heeled shoes. "How'd it go?" I said, flopping down beside her on the couch.

She seemed to sink a couple more inches into the cushions. "Fine," she said, anything but overjoyed. She used the TV control to flick on some talk show, the kind with a bunch of conservatively dressed people in molded plastic seats. "Just great. . . . Did you get Aunt Carrie's card?"

"Yeah."

"Where is it?"

"In the kitchen." She rolled her eyes. "Hey, Mom," I said, "Buck's going to be eating here tonight, all right? Mom, Buck. Buck, Mom." That was my introduction. Mom gave him a warm hi, and he managed to give one back.

She wasn't so warm toward me. "You'll have to fix something yourself," she informed me. "I wasn't planning on cooking."

"Fine with me," I said, and I meant it. Every once in a while—well, once or twice a week, maybe—Mom decides she doesn't want to cook. So the rest of us eat sandwiches or leftovers or something, or Mom calls Dad at the office and asks him to pick something up. Those times are great by me because I can eat what I want when I want without anybody staring at my food and nagging me to eat more, which my mother has a habit of doing.

And wouldn't you know, little brother Bill picked then to decide to come home and strut into the den to see what everyone was doing. He punched me in the shoulder, which was his way of saying hi. I gave him a look but didn't do anything. The best way to handle him is to ignore him.

Bill gave Buck an offhand once-over meant to be tough. "You're new around here," he said.

"You have good eyes," said Buck calmly, smil-

20

ing just a little. He saw right away that Bill was attempting to be smart, and he wasn't letting it get to him.

Bill's head dropped some. He couldn't think of anything to say to that. It was an enjoyable moment for me, to see Bill quiet like that.

"I'm Buck," he said a second later, ruining a great little victory. "You Rich's brother?"

Bill's head lifted. Not quite as high as before, but it was up there. He grinned. "Yeah. Bill."

"Glad to meet you."

"Same here." I could tell Bill thought Buck was "somebody who counts." He turned to Mom. "What's to eat?"

Mom's eyes stayed glued to the talk show, something about May-December romances. "Anything you find in the fridge—as long as you make for yourself."

Gravel crunched under tires in our driveway just after she said that, and Bill took his mind off the prospect of having to feed himself long enough to run to the front door to see who it was. "It's Dad," he announced. "Maybe he'll grill hamburgers."

Mom frowned and looked at her watch. "He's a little early. I hope nothing happened."

"This is Friday," I said. "He's always early on Friday."

"Oh." She looked confused. "Okay."

Bill was already out the door. I heard him harp about hamburgers. Dad nodded as he came in, which meant he was going to do it. He set down his attaché and headed straight to my mother and kissed her. He started to poke her ribs—Mom's really ticklish—but she said "Bill" in that warning tone that meant "not now." Dad backed off, and that's when he saw Buck. He was a little off guard, but not much. He stuck out his hand. "I'm

Mr. Candy," he said, direct and nice, though a little brisk. "You don't belong to me, do you? Who are you?"

Buck took his hand and shook it. "Buck. Buck Dawson."

That was the first time I'd heard Buck's last name. "Buck's staying here tonight," I explained.

"Pleased to have you," said Dad. "Like hamburgers?"

Buck looked sideways at me, and those golden brown eyes were laughing. "Love them," he said.

Dad went upstairs and showered and changed and then came back down. He tied on this "I'm the Chef" apron he'd gotten as a birthday present from a sister-in-law and marched us all out on the back porch to start the serious business of grilling hamburgers. He wouldn't let anyone come near him once he started; he would brandish his spatula in the air like some samurai sword if we tried to see how the burgers were coming along. He was in a great mood; he had Christy and Bill trotting back and forth between the kitchen and picnic table with paper plates and napkins and stuff, and he set Buck and me to slicing tomatoes and chopping onions. Buck was a little bit at a loss with all this, but I just set some tomatoes in front of him and stuck a knife in his hand and started in on my onions.

When Dad had inspected everything and pronounced it up to par, we all dove into the first place at the table we could grab, even Mom, who had lost a little bit of her day's-work exhaustion and was starting to enjoy herself.

Unfortunately, this left Buck standing there with his hands in his pockets, biting his lip. I felt kind of stupid. "Uh—" I started.

Dad broke in. "We're all pigs here," he said

22

heartily. "Very informal. Just jump right in the old trough."

Buck smiled and sat down beside me on the right.

I watched him out of the corner of my eye. He took second and third and even fourth helpings of everything. This didn't faze my parents in the least, though. They were used to my jock friends and their perpetually empty stomachs, and Dad liked nothing better, really, than to get up and flourish his spatula and show off his cooking expertise.

Pretty soon everything edible was eaten. Mom went inside and brought out an old shopping bag and corraled all of us—even Bill, who hates to clean anything—into helping her. Buck was still quiet, held back; he fit right in, and the garbage got picked up twice as fast with just one extra set of hands there.

Then Bill mumbled something about practicing guitar at Jay's, and Christy begged to go to Missy's house. So five minutes later, it was just Mom and Dad and Buck and me, and we all sat around the table there on the deck out back and took in summer.

Casually, out of the blue, Dad said, "I don't remember seeing you around before, Buck. Not that that means anything. Sometimes I forget what my own kids look like." He had lit up his first cigarette of the evening, and he blew smoke at the hedge and didn't crack a smile.

I would've laughed at that poker face of his, but I was in a kind of panic, thinking about how to cover up those innocently dangerous words.

"Well, I'm not from around here, really," said Buck.

I couldn't believe he'd said that. Now the questions would start.

"So where you from?" said Dad predictably. He tapped ashes into the grass.

"Penncrest," I started to say. Penncrest was a rival school district. But Buck looked at me out of the corner of his eyes and gave me a barely perceptible shake of the head. My words died in my throat. this was going to be it, and there was nothing that could stop it.

Buck looked down and away, studying the browning grass on our lawn. He licked his lips. "No," he said, "don't say anything, Rich. It'll come out sooner or later, and it might as well be sooner." He drew a deep breath and looked directly at my parents. Unwavering golden brown animal eyes caught theirs. "You've never seen me around here," he said, "because I'm from L.A. I just met Rich today." He didn't say anything about the tape deck, for which I was deeply thankful.

"I guess I'm what you'd call a runaway," he continued, smiling a little. He paused, but my parents didn't say a word. They were very grave and very intent. "Because that's what I did," he went on. "I couldn't stay where I was. . . . I didn't have anywhere to go. My mother died a while ago. . . . I didn't want anybody taking me anywhere. . . . Don't feel sorry for me. I did what I wanted to do. Look, just let me stay here tonight, just tonight. . . . Don't try to take me somewhere. . . . It won't work. . . . And don't blame Rich. He was just being decent. . . ."

He kept taking little pants between phrases, and when he was done, he half rose from the bench like he meant to run off right then and there.

My dad said, "Sit down, Buck."

His voice was very tired.

Let me tell you about my parents. They're naggers, and they're inescapably suburban, and way

24

down deep they're the most generous people in the world.

My mother volunteers at the hospital and at an old-folks' home, on top of her full-time job. Together, she and my father support at least a half-dozen charities. Neither of them can turn down anyone, and the only reason our house isn't crawling with stray mutts and kittens is because they're both so good at recruiting homes for them.

Buck had the same effect on them as he had on me. There was something in him that made them want to help him. So they helped.

They offered Buck a home. Buck had no family, and the law wouldn't allow him to live on his own. Though Buck persistently threatened to run away if my parents went to the authorities, it finally got through his head that that was the only way he could keep this place that was offered him for his last year in high school. So, in the end, he gave in. He was glad to, I think. Running had worn him to the bone. He was tired, and he didn't have room to pretend he'd rather go on.

There were a lot of long, involved, tedious legal and social procedures, procedures that were dinner-table topics for the rest of the summer. But long before any papers were finalized, it was finalized in our home that Buck would become part of the family.

This was all fine and great, but I have to admit that at first I was a little worried. After all, what did we know about this guy? Sure, he was nice and he was warm and he was eager and more than willing to work for his keep, but I hadn't forgotten about the tape deck. And even though I kept it in a locked file way in the back of my memory, I couldn't help thinking every once in a while about what he'd told me in the car on the way home that first day I'd met him.

25

But there was that bond between us. Buck was a brother to me, a buddy. I wouldn't hold his past against him, not when it was so obvious how badly he wanted and needed a real chance.

It was still summer, too, the very last days of summer, not a time to ruin with worrying. My senior year was days away; I had a grateful live-in best friend who went out of his way to fit in; I had absolutely nothing to complain about, except having to share my room again.

And then school started.

Chapter 3

So here it was, the first day of my—and Buck's—last year in high school. It really wasn't that exciting. The first day of first grade is so exciting it terrorizes you, and it goes downhill fast from there.

Buck and I were in the same homeroom, I in the second seat in the first row and he in the third-to-last seat in the second row, according to alphabetical order. I left him to himself—he'd told me he wanted to float on his own rather than depend on me to take him through the social maze. That was fine with me. I wouldn't have minded showing him around, but relying on himself was a lot better for him, I thought.

So I minded my own business. Talked to a few casual buddies, complained about teachers and classes, flirted a little. But out of the corner of my eye I was watching for reactions to Buck; I was careful to listen, in case anybody said anything. I guess I was interested in how my protégé was doing. Really, I should have minded my own business. But he was out on the proving ground, and I was watching because I was hoping he'd do well by me.

He was causing a reaction, all right, and this was just a little unusual.

See, usually people are pretty indifferent to somebody new. I mean, they're friendly enough and casually interested, but mostly they don't care. They're already set in their own social niches. They have their friends, and those friends belong to a certain group, and that's the way it goes. A nicheless person isn't someone to be concerned with. It's much more important to concentrate on staying where you're at or maybe even moving in the direction that looks like up.

But Buck was getting looks, second and third and fourth glances, and not just from girls. They were from everyone. People were asking each other who he was. As a matter of fact, I was asked at least twice. "Who's that kid back there? He new?"

And I would say, "Yeah, he's new. His name's Buck Dawson—he lives with us." And people would look at me in a little different light—a respectful light. That made me feel good, proud ... almost as if I'd done something really important.

You can label a lot of people. Label them prep, jock, nerd, punk. The labels have a lot to do with looks. You dress like your group. Regular clothes might as well be uniforms. You can walk down the hall and label just about everyone who goes by, and your labels will probably be right.

But there was no label for Buck. Labels slid from him like water from wax. They just didn't stick. He was one of a kind, and whatever that kind was, it didn't have a name.

He wore a blue flannel shirt that stretched tight

across his shoulders. This would have marked him as what we called a burnout, the addict type, the flunking troublemaker who skipped classes to smoke dope in the bathroom. But his shirt was buttoned, not hanging open to show off a grimy old death's-head T-shirt. His sleeves were rolled up to just under the elbow, sort of like a farmer, and he didn't have any bandannas or chains hanging off a leather belt with about fifty keys attached to them. He had Nike high-tops on his feet, not heavy old army boots, and his jeans were jock in style, snug and new, not bleached and frayed and baggy.

No, he wasn't a burnout. But he wasn't a jock, either. He was too aloof for that.

People looked at him once and twice and again and still couldn't place him. He didn't follow any identifiable social code. He was noble and alert and liquid as a twelve-point stag on a spring morning, and as elusive and magnetic. Everything about him was tawny—his hair, his eyes, his attitude. And that tawniness made him stand out in a quietly powerful way. The best people could do was figure he must've been something pretty big at his old school—how could he not be?

Oh, he was causing a stir with that look of his, all right. And even though he sat there unprepossessing and nice, from clear across the room I could feel a touch of smugness coming from deep behind those carefully amiable and noncommittal eyes. He knew that attention was for him, and he liked it.

I didn't see Buck again—besides passing him in the halls once or twice, which I acknowledged with a small lift of the head—until sixth-period study hall.

I was one of the first ones in the room, so I

picked myself a seat and sat down, watching to see who would come in the room. It was the usual mix.

Quite a few burnouts showed up. They have a lot of study halls because they only have about two other classes, the required ones. They all, guys and girls alike, wore the same torn flannel shirts with the old T-shirts underneath and beat-up jeans and boots or maybe tennis shoes a bag lady wouldn't wear. They all slouched in with sullen or spaced-out looks on their faces—or what you could see of their faces under a foot of stringy hair. They didn't seem to have much of an opinion of this particular study hall, not mumbling much more than "Who gives a f——?" Then again, that was their opinion of everything. They didn't care, so they didn't make distinctions. They were lost in themselves, and they were scared, so they covered it with loud violent mouths and tough mean acts and ugly indifferent attitudes. They kept to themselves and boiled among themselves, daring the world to care enough to do something to them.

Three or four of the social types bounced in shoulder-to-shoulder in a little clutch, laughing in high voices and discussing which teachers they could get hall passes from. I didn't know any of them personally, but it was a sure bet all of them were probably involved in at least five different extracurricular activities like class government and Future Business Leaders of America nd the yearbook and that kind of thing. They grouped up in a front corner, pushing their desks together and pulling mirrors and mascara out of their purses and straightening their coordinated sweaters and skirts. They were oblivious to the rest of the room, happy with organizing their alphabet-soup clubs and dances and fund-raisers and happy with their prospective good grades and fun times in class.

Then there were some jocks—my type, I guess you could say—who ambled in and just kind of congregated in the middle of the room, since the burnouts had all the seats in the back. These were the guys I knew, and we said the regular things like "Hey, how ya doin'," or "Wha'sup?" or any other of a bunch of dumb-mouthed phrases. We were the guys who ruled the school, and we knew it. We had out tight jeans or tight black pants and our sharp designer shirts and maybe a gold chain, and we looked good with our muscles and our status, and we didn't mind showing all this off. We had a female complement to our group, the cheerleaders and the homecoming-court types—they moved with the socials but had extra status because they went with jocks. Yeah, we were the biggest and the best, and we wouldn't let anyone forget it.

Sure, the social structure could be tough, with its castes and cliques and all those unwritten rules you just don't break if you know what's good for you. You're stuck with a label, and all you can do is conform with it. Burnout, with no way out. Social, pretty, and popular, usually airheaded too, although some of the socials were pretty solid and responsible. Brain, not acknowledged as human because of thick glasses and four-point-zero grade averages. Nerd, too reserved for burnout, too weird and stumbling for social, not smart enough for brain—the nowhere people. And jock—rulers of the school, cool and sure, and as limited by the categories they kept everyone in as the people in the categories themselves.

But I was jock—not a major, king-of-the-school kind of jock, but nonetheless jock—and I had it good. There was nothing I wanted to change.

Just as the bell rang, Tony Marinelli strolled in with those long, strutting strides of his, head

31

high, grinning like a tomcat. He kind of swept his eyes around the room, decided I was the best guy present to socialize with, and moved right on over to sit beside me.

Tony was what you could call king of the jocks, leader of the pack. Tony didn't answer to anybody. There was no one who would seriously cross him, but he could cross anybody he pleased because he was top of the scale. He was domineering and he had a proud, awful temper.

Tony was an all-round jock. You name it, he was into it, and he was good at it. His specialty was football, though, and believe me, he had definite makings of a pro.

But he was an amiable enough guy, even if he was arrogant and mirror-bound. He had a great sense of humor, when he felt like being humorous. He could make you laugh about a broken leg even as you were moaning in pain because yours was the leg that was broken. I know, because it happened to a guy named Tom Lydell during practice last fall. Tony was the one to keep him calm until the ambulance came.

And Tony had this great sense of, well, chivalry, that not too many guys these days have. He opened doors for girls and never swore around them. He treated his junior-prom-queen girl friend, Tina Pierce, like a glass goddess; he was sincere about it too. It wasn't a joke.

Tony was jock to the bone, jock with all his heart and soul and body. There were some other jocks who were just as jock as Tony, but they were uglier or dumber or less talented or less dynamic or less outgoing or less dominant than Tony, and came across like losers because of it.

Jock wasn't necessarily synonymous with winner.

So Tony sat down beside me and said, "Hey,

Candyman, how's it goin'?" Candyman is a jock nickname I had.

I asked him about a mutual buddy, Rex Grant, who'd been jumped just a week and a half ago by a bunch of burnouts, wondering if we planned a return on that. But before I got an answer, Buck walked in.

I swear, heads turned. The social girls in the front corner giggled, and one of them called hi. Buck smiled at them, not studsy the way Tony would've, but just nice. Tony leaned across the aisle, Tina's class ring swinging on its gold chain around his neck, and aid to me, "I think that golden boy there is new. He's in my algebra class...third period."

I said, "Yeah, he's new. He lives with me."

Tony's eyebrows arched. "Yeah? How come I didn't hear about it?"

Tony was used to knowing about everything.

"Well, hey, you can't hear it all," I said, enjoying myself. But then I saw the dark hint of a frown and amended, "You know, I've been busy with the job and all...he just came, y'know...didn't think to mention it to you."

Buck came and sat down in front of Tony, diagonal to me, easy and comfortable as anything. He didn't say a word, but those golden brown eyes caught mine, and right then and there I knew he knew what Tony was and that he wasn't impressed by it in the least. I had to look away from those eyes because I didn't want Tony to see what they were saying reflected in me.

Tony twisted around in his seat so he could face me and Buck at the same time. "So," he said to Buck, raising his chin a little, "aren't you in my algebra class?"

"Yeah, Tony," Buck said seriously, unsmiling. "You're in my class."

There were tiny accents on *you're* and *my*. Suddenly, I was really uncomfortable. I hoped Tony wouldn't pick up on Buck's inflection. I looked at Buck with knitted brows; I couldn't understand why he was being antagonistic.

I shouldn't have worried. Right after he came up with that, Buck went on to say, "Hey . . . I heard you quarterbacked a championship game last year."

Buck had gone straight for Tony's vain spot and hit it on the nose. Tony leaned back and gave a sleepy kind of shrug and an even sleepier laugh and started with, "I didn't do that much, really. . . ." And he went on with the old self-love story from there.

Buck laughed at all the right times and came up with a lot of candid remarks Tony honestly appreciated—they were close to the kind of thing he would've said himself. Pretty soon they were rapping about all kinds of stuff, and Buck—and I—got invited to a party I myself had only just found out about.

Buck had made an impression—again.

And I was glad that Buck fit in so well with so little trouble.

That night at home we had a big family dinner with all of us eating at the same time. Mom had had a day off, and she'd made spaghetti, a big pot of it. She'd made salad and garlic bread too. She'd spent a lot of time on it, and it was great.

Dad brought up the old question "How was the first day back?" as soon as he'd slurped up his last strand of spaghetti, which was long before anyone else. Dad's a fast eater.

Christy took that as a cue. She set down her fork and launched into a speech about how Mrs. Pender was the meanest sixth-grade teacher in the whole world and how she and Missy had to sit on opposite sides of the room and how unfair it was that Miss O'Connor's class got to paint the windows of their room and they didn't.

Mom and Dad responded to those woes with a sympathy that was only very faintly dry, and Bill infuriated Christy with a mumbled, "Whoooo caaaares." I just kept chipping away at the mountain of spaghetti on my plate and smiled.

The spotlight turned on Bill next, and of course nobody could pry anything out of him except, "I got homework already. School's school, all right?"

Dad gave up on Bill. "How about you two?" he said, turning to me and Buck. Dad and Mom were always very careful—too careful, I thought—to never put one of us before the other. I guess they didn't want any jealousy cropping up.

I shrugged. I really didn't have anything to say. "Same as always," I offered after a minute.

Buck had raised his eyebrows and was starting to say something when the phone rang.

"Probably for me," Bill said before the first ring even finished.

We were eating in the kitchen, and the kitchen phone is mounted on the wall right above where I sit, so I reached over my head to get it, swallowing a mouthful of pasta in a hurry so I wouldn't sound like a pig.

"Hello?" I said.

"Hi." It was a girl. I didn't recognize the voice. "Is Buck there?"

The first day, and he already had a call. I must've been surprised because I said, "What's that?"

"Is Buck there?"

"Uh...hang on a minute." I covered the receiver with my hand. "Lady admirer for you, Buck."

Everybody stared at him. He had this weird

35

expression, as if something very funny had just happened and he wanted to laugh but was trying to hold it back to be polite.

Solemnly, Christy said, "Do you mean it's a girl?"

"Take it upstairs," I told him. "Take the hall phone into our room."

He obeyed without a word, pushing back his chair and standing up and turning to go upstairs as if he was sightly dazed.

"Hurry up," I told him.

I stayed on until I heard him pick up the extension and say, "Hello?" Then I hung up and went back to my spaghetti. It wasn't until a few seconds later that I noticed the expectant looks.

I shrugged again. "That's how his whole day went," I said. "Just like that."

Buck stayed on the phone a good half-hour, maybe more. Don't ask me how he thought of enough to say to some girl who was practically a total stranger to fill all that time, but he did it just like he did everything else—cool and comfortable and easy.

I went up to my room after about twenty minutes to find a cassette of Bill's I'd borrowed. Of course, both Buck and I knew that I was up there to listen to what he was saying, but he wasn't mad or even annoyed, so I decided to stick around until he was done.

It was funny to watch him. He was on his back on Bill's old bed that we'd brought up from the basement for him, and he had one leg braced against the all and the telephone cord wrapped around his wrist. He kept pulling on it, pulling it and letting it spring back.

Finally, he said good-bye, went out in the hall to hang up the phone, and as soon as he came back he said, "Colleen Burgett," which ticked me off slightly because he knew exactly what I had been dying to ask. Even so, hearing that name made me curious and a little bruised. Colleen was a social girl, one of Tina Pierce's cronies, and if things went the same for her as they had the last two years, she'd be class VP again. I'd sort of made a play for her the year before—she was pretty and bubbly—but she was busy all the time and was cool to me. I was a jock, but like I said, not really a major one.

I settled for going on to my next question. "What'd she want?"

His face got that same funny look as before. "To talk."

"What for?" I wanted to know. My attitude was a little harsh because I was busy ignoring the girl who'd ignored me for three years had called Buck the first day she met him, and at my own number at that.

"Oh, some kind of bull about me being perfect for some kind of committee head or something."

At least he could tell it was bull. There was hope. "Sure," I scoffed. I went on with something really crude about what it was she really wanted from him.

Buck laughed. Then he said, "You got nothing to worry about, Rich. She called me, not the other way around. And I told her I didn't have the time to be on any committee...."

For some reason, I felt a whole lot better.

Chapter 4

If no other guy in my high school society was quite as jockish as Tony Marinelli, no other burnout was quite as burnt as Buzz McKinney.

Buzz wasn't Buzz's real name. His real name was William. I don't know why they called him Buzz. All I know is he'd been called that for as long as anyone could remember.

Buzz had been suspended so many times that he was out of school more often than he was in. It was a wonder he hadn't been expelled for some of the things he'd done, and it was more of a wonder he hadn't just quit. Teachers hated him because he was belligerent, obnoxious, and unbelievably crude, not to mention downright dangerous. I think he might have invented a few original cusswords in his time. He was pretty good-sized and rocky but not heavy or brutish, and I don't think he ever respected anyone or anything in his life. He would've spit on the Pope if the

Pope happened to be in the same direction as he spit.

And he was smart. Sure, he flunked just about every class he ever took—including phys ed, which is a near impossibility—only to be promoted each year by teachers who couldn't stand the thought of facing him again. But he was smart. Flunking classes was a point of honor, a point against the system and social conformity.

Maybe he had a terrible home life. Probably, he did. But an inherent viciousness took him beyond what most burnouts were. He was soaked in bad, and he liked it.

He used his smart to make himself into the biggest underground supplier in high school, and his ring extended into the junior highs and the neighborhoods where the kids lived. And his supplies weren't limited to pot and ludes. He could get you anything you weren't supposed to have if you made it worth his time.

Let me give an insight into his character. He would even do business with jocks if the price was right.

Buck got over on Buzz.

It was the third week of school. Things had been smooth as silk up until then, with Buck establishing himself good and firm with me and my crew, going to parties and impressing everyone with his cool wisped haircut that wasn't quite New Wave and his tawny, vulnerable charm. He ate lunch with my buddies, and still everyone was coming up to me and telling me what a great guy Buck was, which made me happy with myself and him too.

This Friday morning of the third week of school, Buck and I were bumming around the halls, leaning against lockers and talking jock bull with whoever came by.

There was a traffic lull, and that's when Buzz chose to swagger by with that despise-the-world walk of his. His head turned. Buck always made heads turn. Buzz's head turned slow and cold, and his eyes were hard and mocking.

Buck did the stupidest thing he could have done. He made eye contact.

You don't make eye contact with people like Buzz. They're mean and snarling as junkyard dogs, and it doesn't take anything to provoke them. Buzz was the type who took everything personally and in the wrong. They say if you stare at certain animals for too long, they'll take it as a signal to attack. Buzz was like that.

He stopped dead in front of Buck, jaw up and level and forward, green eyes flat. "You looking at something, man?" Buzz was looking for a fight, and I knew it. It didn't take much of a brain to see when a guy wanted to pick a fight; when that guy was Buzz, you backed off.

Buck had the supreme stupidity to keep staring and say, "Sure I'm looking at something. Question is, Is it something I want to be looking at?"

Buzz grabbed that with all his teeth. He moved a step closer, close enough to jab Buck in the chest, which is exactly what he did. Buck didn't pay any attention to it. His eyes never left Buzz's.

I was getting worried. Buck wasn't burnout, and he'd identified himself with jock. In Buzz's mind that's what he was—jock. Burnouts don't like jocks, and Buzz was no exception to the rule. He didn't just dislike jocks, he hated them. He hated them because even though he didn't care about high school society, he hated the fact that he didn't rule it; that because of who he was, he was looked down on and despised by everyone but his cronies, and especially by jocks.

Buzz said—snarled is more like it—"It better be, fag."

My guts went cold when I heard that. Something was going to explode.

Fury poured into Buck's eyes. The golden brown was molten.

By this time a few people had stopped and were becoming one of those circles that always form around a flight. And there I was in the middle of it going crazy from not knowing what to do.

Buck did something then that nobody had ever done before. He grabbed a handful of Buzz's flannel shirt and jerked him closer to him than he already was. The crowd instinctively fell back a little, and I moved a half step with it. I was scared, but it was out of my hands, and I wasn't about to get myself killed because of Buck's mouth.

A real fight should've started right there. Buzz should've gone for Buck then and there like he would've gone for anyone else who handled him like that. But he didn't. He just stared up at Buck—Buck had an inch or two on him—sort of caught in mid-snarl.

The crowd held its breath. It was the quietest fight I'd ever seen.

It was Buck's eyes that stopped Buzz. I don't know what Buzz read in them, but whatever it was, it got him cold. A little bit of that same chill came my way, and I was looking at Buck like I'd never seen him before.

Very softly, voice oddly lilting, Buck said, "It better be, huh? Let me tell you something. Don't you ever, ever make the mistake of thinking there's nobody around tougher than you. Because if you do, you'll learn awful fast how wrong you are, and you'll learn in a way that hurts, man."

Nobody had expected something like that, least of all Buzz. Fighting back was the only reaction he knew. And what Buck said made him uncomfortable—like he wasn't used to being. And being uncomfortable and confused made him mad. I could see the mad building up in his face.

Maybe something would've happened then, with Buzz mad like that, but by this time a couple of teachers, Mr. Flynn and Mr. Carter, were bulldozing the crowd, breaking it up and scattering it.

"Get to homeroom! Back to homeroom!"

Most people left in a hurry, not wanting to get in trouble and itching to spread the news. But I sort of slid down the row of lockers a few feet, waiting to see what would happen.

Buck and Buzz were already separated—they'd never actually been fighting, after all—but Mr. Flynn pushed them farther apart. Mr. Flynn was short and chunky but tough as lead—he was the wrestling coach—so Buzz didn't give him any trouble.

Mr. Flynn was really mad. He stood there with his bulldog jaw stuck out like he was going to belt both of them right there. But all he did was demand in this weird calm voice, "All right, what's going on here, boys?" Then he happened to glance just past Buck to some of Buzz's cronies hovering in the background. He wasn't so calm then. "Back to homeroom!" he yelled, sweeping his arm at them. "Go! Now!" He turned back over his shoulder and saw me. "You too, Candy! Vamoose!"

I had to go then, but before I went I took a last look at Buck, and Buck saw me and smiled. All the fury was gone. He looked...smug, almost triumphant.

* * *

I had to wait until sixth-period study hall to find out what happened next.

I was early, like always. The burnouts came in and eyed me as they slouched to the back of the room, and the first thing my jock buddies did after they filtered in the door was come to me and say, "Hey, hear about Buck?" or "Hey, you hear about the fight?" or "What happened with Buck?" and so on. I kept as quiet as I could for Buck's sake, not wanting to spread anything around.

It was hard. Tony came in and pressed me for everything I had with everything he had. "But what happened?" he kept asking. "C'mon, Candy. What happened?" I swear Tony was worse than one of those gabby social girls when it came to wanting to know what was going on.

Buck came in late, like always, and there weren't a pair of eyes in the whole room that weren't on him except mine — which were on everyone else. I was trying to pick up a general reaction, but it was hard to find. There was mostly an eagerness in the air, a curiosity, a waiting.

Apparently oblivious to everything, Buck slid into his seat cool and calm as a cat. Tony was on him in a second.

"Hey, Buck," he said. Dryly, I wondered why he even bothered to put on the casual act. "How's it goin'?"

"Fine," said Buck blithely.

Tony paused to think. "Heard you had a run-in today," he said, talking like he was discussing the weather.

"Yeah. I did. Buzz McKinney," said Buck. He matched Tony's nonchalance stride for stride, and did it with a straight face too.

Tony waited until it was almost mockingly clear that Buck wasn't going to be pulled into the game. His temper arched its back. He smiled as he leaned

44

back but his eyes were darker than usual and a little glittery. "Well, let's hear it, Dawson," he told Buck. Told, not asked.

Buck shrugged. "Buzz came up to me after homeroom," he said. I'll bet you that whole room was listening in. "And we said a couple things, y'know? And that's about it."

"I heard you went to the vice," prodded Tony sharply.

"Oh yeah. Well, that was no big deal. He gave me a warning and gave Buzz detention. It wasn't fair, really—"

"Sure it was fair," interrupted Tony. "All McKinney does is make trouble. He deserves whatever he gets. It blows my mind that he hasn't got himself kicked in jail yet. I'll tell you what, Buck. You better watch out from here on. Mc-Kinney's scum, real live dirt-eating scum, and he'll be out for you."

Buck just raised an eyebrow. "Scum?" he said. "What makes you call him scum?"

Tony swore under his breath, then glanced at old Mrs. Weber at her desk in the front of the room. She was fiddling away with a stack of papers; she hadn't noticed a thing.

"C'mon," said Tony, really angry. "You defending him?"

"I'm not defending him. I just asked a question."

"You were defending him. Don't do that," warned Tony, and he was dead serious. "He's scum. He's gotten a lot of people in a lot of trouble. He pushes everything from A to Z and at a high price too."

They kept dueling like that, and a feeling something close to ice water trickling down the back of my neck crept over me.

Buck was studying the top of his desk. "I'm not saying what Buzz does is any good," he said care-

45

fully. Tony's mouth was tight, but he was listening. "I don't like it. What I'm saying is that that's a *person* you're calling scum. Don't judge what he does before you know the reason behind it. Judge him for what he *is*."

"He's scum," insisted Tony, those big muscles of his all corded and tight. "And he does what he does because he's scum."

"You have no idea what he is," retorted Buck. He was losing some of his calm despite himself. "I bet you never said more than two words to him." He went on to describe all the words Tony probably used. "I'll tell you something. I talked to him; believe it or not, he's human just like me and maybe you."

That got me, all right. Had he actually managed to pull the on-and-off flattery trick on Buzz too? It was hard to believe. Buzz was too bitter to respond to it. Unless Buck had squeezed a little respect from somewhere in Buzz, just enough so he would talk to the jock who'd put him down. Maybe, just maybe.

I thought now was a good time to interfere. The interest in the room was peaking too high. The burnouts in the back were alive for once, watching a jock defend them. And the jocks were watching Buck and Tony with a confused curiosity, a curiosity bordering danger.

I stretched a grin straight across my face and tilted my chair back. "Hey, fight nice, kids," I said lightly. "Think about tonight."

That did the trick. The prospect of cruising and getting drunk and staying out way too late on a Friday night was too good to ignore. And then, thank God, Buck did the right thing. He pushed Tony's shoulder and said, "Hey. Didn't mean to get on you like that. It's just the whole thing, y'know, everybody getting on me with questions everywhere I go."

Tony smiled. Apology made, order—his order—restored, he was happy again. "Yeah, yeah, I know, I push it too hard," he said generously.

"Don't we all," said Buck.

So everybody was friends again and everything was all right.

For a while, anyway.

Chapter 5

Cruising and drinking are what you could call the established weekend pastimes of the jocks and the burnouts. The only difference between the two groups was that the burnouts also operated during the week, while jocks sometimes had curfews or games and that kind of thing.

I first started drinking around fourteen, I guess. Seven years before the legal age. It's not something I'm exactly proud of, but I'm not going to pretend I think it's a terrible crime, either. Everybody did it, and nobody made a big deal about it. And I was careful. I never drove when I drank, and I didn't make a habit of blowing my mind on a weekly basis like some guys did.

I used to hate it—the drinking, I mean—when I first started. Beer's kind of bitter, and it still isn't my favorite thing. But I'm used to it now. I guess I even like it.

I justify it to myself like this. I don't smoke, don't do drugs, don't mug people, don't chew, don't fight, don't get girls pregnant, don't shoplift, don't do anything off a whole book of don'ts that get done anyway by a lot of people. Why can't I have just one little don't? One black mark?

Like I always say, who's perfect?

Not me, and I'll be the first to admit it.

Anyway, about drinking. My parents knew I drank. They didn't approve, but they didn't disapprove. They just figured it was my own decision, and they probably also figured I'd do it anyway even if they told me not to.

I've come home drunk and been caught. When I do get caught, I really go through the grinder. I'll never forget this one time at the beginning of summer—about two months before Buck showed up—when I staggered in at four in the morning as close to dead drunk as I've ever been. Like I said, I don't usually go overboard, but there had been these end-of-school celebrations that had gotten out of hand....

And there was Dad in his bathrobe, standing in the door with a book in his hand and red in his eyes. His lips were tight, and that would've made me cringe if I hadn't been too gone to see it.

Well, he steamrolled me. Not that I didn't deserve it, but he was really hard on me, and me feeling like I was in an elevator rushing up about a hundred miles an hour. After he was done with me, he took me to my room and left me in bed, where I stayed until three-thirty in the afternoon. He never said another word about that little episode. I guess he didn't have to, because I never got drunk like that again, and I don't think I'll try to in the future.

And not once had Dad said I couldn't drink.

So, like I said, cruising and drinking were the favorite pastimes of those who ruled the school;

after the game on Friday night—the same Friday when Buck got over on Buzz—that's exactly what Buck and I were doing.

We were on our way to this field that was about a five-minute drive down the road from school, Buck at the wheel—he'd just gotten his permit—and me with a six-pack between my feet. This field was flat and out of the way and the grass was thick and not more than a foot tall with not too many weeds. The edges of the field were screened with a lot of scrubby trees, which made it a perfect place for getting drunk. Which made it a favorite place with the drinking crowd—the jock drinking crowd. And since I was a member of the jock crowd, I was on my way to that field just like every other jock who could find a way to get there.

Buck almost missed the dirt-road pull-off, but he managed to veer into it—at about forty miles an hour, which almost threw me out of the car and could've killed us—before he passed it. He took the car as far back as he could and then parked it.

Four or five cars were already back there, which meant a pretty big group would be gathered tonight. I grabbed my six-pack and motioned Buck out of the car and headed down the path through the trees.

I'd been right about the number of people that I guessed would be there. I could tell this would be a wild night. There was Don Pressman with his newest out-of-town girlfriend. There were the three inseparable stooges of the jock crowd, Jack Sempsey and Mike Dubrow and Trace Kemp. My buddy Rex was there, along with Bob Cordero and Kip Mason and Jeff Gradowski. Mixed in with them were Steph Allen—the sleaziest cheerleader I've ever met—and a whole bunch of her jockette-type cronies.

Kip Mason ambled over to me as I melted in and said, "Wha'ja bring?"

I held up the six-pack.

"Zat it?" he demanded genially.

I shrugged and smiled.

"S'okay," he offered. "Jack's gotta case."

"Good," I said automatically with an automatic grin. But I was thinking about what a jerk Kip was and wondering how much of his slur was an act. Kip had a way of exaggerating everything, including the effect of alcohol on his brain. More than once I'd caught him faking it. He used drunk as an excuse to do things he wanted to do but knew people would think were really weird if he weren't drunk.

Anyway, Kip concluded his near-pointless conversation with, "have an extra one for me," and left.

Buck had already been corraled by Steph and one of her friends. I silently wished him luck and found Rex. He wasn't drunk at all. Ever since he'd been jumped and gotten that face he was so proud of all bruised up, he'd been awful careful to keep himself under control.

"Where's Tony?" I wanted to know. I'd noticed that the star of the show was missing.

"I d'know," was Rex's concerned reply. "Crying in the locker room, I bet."

I frowned and started to ask what he meant by that, but then I remembered. We'd lost the game, lost it at 0-21. It was the first game of the season including exhibition that we'd lost.

Tony hated losing. He took losing personally. He was ashamed of losing, and shame was something that bit him deep. Rex was probably speaking more truth than he knew when he said Tony was crying in the locker room.

* * *

By the time Tony showed up, I was deep into my sixth can and also deep into playing the game with Debbie Townes.

Debbie Townes was blond and dark-eyed, with a look you could call cuddly. She wasn't what you'd label "bad girl," but she wasn't a "good girl," either. She was a friend of Steph Allen's, and that says it all. But she was nice enough to talk to on a Friday night when you were drunk, and that's what I was doing. Talking—and playing the game.

You know how it goes. Everybody's played it. You hint, you use a lot of double meanings, you smile a lot, and all the time you get closer and closer and try for a little more and a little more and then some more. The game ends when the fun stops, and that part's always up to the girl. But the girl's in a lot of trouble if the guy decides he isn't going to follow her rules.

Sometimes the game can last for months, and sometimes for a half-hour. The Friday-night game I was playing was in the hour category—those Friday games usually are. We'd kissed a few times, and then some. And Debbie was showing no signs of ending the game.

But then Tony showed up.

Debbie sat up in the grass and watched him swallow beer and lean against Rex and feel sorry for himself. "Poor Tony," she said a little unclearly.

Tony was subdued. That's the only word for it. Subdued. He was exhausted and he had lost his game and he looked like he really might have been crying. I wondered where Tina was. Maybe she was sick or something. Maybe if she'd been there Tony would have been in better shape.

Anyway, Tony was looking for something— sympathy, I guess—to ease his shame. He wanted to be told he was wonderful and the best, and his wanting showed in the way he was so subdued, the way he kept close to Rex.

To tell the truth, I didn't care. I didn't care about Tony or what Tony was doing. At the moment, me and my body were deep into the game and didn't want to be disturbed. To be honest, I was taking advantage of Debbie's not being exactly a "good girl" for totally selfish reasons—my own pleasure and satisfaction. I couldn't have cared less about her feelings or her reasons for playing the game, just as long as she continued to play. As soon as she ended the game, I would've walked away and never looked back.

I only get that way—cruel and indifferent and raunchy—when I'm drunk. Don't ask me why.

I was deep in beer anyway, and deep in the game, when Tony showed. I wouldn't have even noticed him if it weren't for Debbie's sitting up and noticing him and if it weren't for what happened next.

What happened next was Buzz.

Headlights cut into the field through the scrubby trees, and a few of us peered through them to the dirt trail to see who was coming. The moon was full and the night was breezy warm and cloudless, but still there wasn't enough light to make out individual features until a person was about five or ten feet away. So nobody knew that the two bodies walking into the field were Buzz McKinney and his pal Joe Parriot until Buzz came within a few feet of the group of us and said, "Where's Buck Dawson?"

I jumped up from Debbie's side like she'd electrocuted me, and I wasn't the only one surprised. Buzz's voice had cut off all the talking and jagging around and had made every head turn, and you could just feel the animosity pouring from a bunch of the guys like Rex and Don Pressman and Kip Mason.

Tony reacted like he'd been slapped. He snapped right out of his subdued mood. This snarl spread across his face, and I swear he would've jumped Buzz right then and there for daring to break into a jock gathering, his gathering, if Buck hadn't said, calm as still water, "Hey, Buzz, thought you weren't going to make it."

That stopped Tony dead, all right, and just about everyone else too. My head was spinning. Now the stares were pinned on Buck, who slid out of Steph's claws and walked over and gave Buzz an easy punch on the shoulder like they'd been friends for years.

To use an old cliché—you could've heard a pin drop.

I remember a tearing, choking sensation pulling at my throat. Somebody is going to end up hurt, I was thinking.

Loudly, very loudly, Debbie said, "Are they friends?" I wanted to kick her and almost did.

Buck pretended not to hear. He turned to Tony. Innocently nonchalant, he said, "Hey, you know each other, right?"

Quickly—too quickly—Buzz said, "Yeah, yeah. We know each other. And we brought that case you asked for. It's in the car...if you want it." Joe Parriot back-shifted. His thin hands were in his pockets where everybody knew he kept that silver-handled blade that was as narrow and metallic and sharp as Joe himself.

Buck prompted Tony. "You want that case, don't you, Marinelli?" He was still pulling that vague, innocent act. And worse, it was working. The jock crowd liked Buck, trusted Buck. And they were drunk and wanted to get drunker.

Tony's mouth hung open. He was caught in an

awful position. He had absolutely no solid reason to be on the defensive. If he put himself on the defensive, he would look bad. And he didn't want to look bad. So he went along with Buck. It was his only choice. He forced a smile and said, "Bring it on."

Tony's crowd saw their king accept the burnout king with a sharp white smile. So they accepted Buzz and Joe too, accepted them without thinking twice. They were too drunk to think twice.

Maybe if somebody had thought twice, things would've turned out a lot different. But nobody thought twice.

Especially not me. I was too interested in getting back to the game to think twice.

That day had started in a bad way, and that weird, messed-up night ended up worse.

Tony got sick. So did Jack and Trace, but that always happened. It was normal. Tony's getting sick was really kind of pitiful.

Debbie quit the game. She played for a while, sure. Just long enough to pull me past the point where the game becomes something more than a game. She'd warmed up to me and then drawn back and cooled off. Warmed up, cooled off, warmed up, cooled off. That kind of treatment will crack stone, and it sure didn't do me any good.

The frustration of it wouldn't have been important, though, except for one thing. It got Buck and me into what you could call a fight.

The after-game fun broke up about an hour after Buzz and Joe brought the second case. To be exact, it broke up when Tony got sick. Rex and Bob Cordero got him up and took him home, and the rest of the jocks filtered away pretty quick after that. Steph and her crew—including Debbie—didn't have any reason to stay once the guys were gone,

56

so they left, too. The last ones to go were Buzz and Joe, and who knows when they left. Buck and I left them standing there close to each other, puffing on joints, and Buzz's good-bye to Buck was flat and intimate.

Buck drove home. He hadn't touched a drop, and I'd known beforehand that he wouldn't. Buck wouldn't go near any booze. He'd told me he never wanted anything besides his own mind influencing his actions, but I think it had more to do with how his mother had been a lush and give him some bad experiences.

So Buck drove home.

He was perfectly awake and in a disgustingly good mood, which put me in a worse mood. I sat there staring out the window, fed up with the whole deal. What was it all for? Why was I stupid enough to fall for playing the game every time? I didn't even have an opinion about Debbie one way or another, but here I was thinking about her—in a physical way. And the more I thought, the more I ached; the more I ached, the more I thought.

It was a vicious circle.

Buck whistled through his teeth with the radio a few minutes. I gritted my teeth at the sound. Then, kind of contemplatively, he said, "I really like that kind of partying. . . . You know?"

I hunched into my jacket. "Uh-huh."

He didn't seem to notice my cool shoulder. "Partying was totally different back there," he went on. "In L.A., I mean. People partied wild there, tried to get as insane as they could—it was bad. Some of it was funny. . . ." He was quiet then. "Sometimes I almost miss it," he said slowly, eyes focused deep and straight on the road ahead. "Don't take that wrong. I love being here. I really do. You know that, Rich. This is the best I've ever had. I got a home, I got friends, I got parties. . . .

Everyone should have it this good. It's not fair that they don't."

I looked sideways at him, him with one strong hand easy on the wheel. "Life's not fair, okay?" I said. "Thinking about it like that won't change anything. Just don't worry about it."

He jabbed the accelerator. The car lurched forward, and I grabbed the dash. "Don't worry about it? You say don't worry about it? Listen. If I didn't worry about it, I'd be dead."

He was harsh and hard, but I was in a rotten state of mind, in no mood to sympathize. "Come off it. You're here now."

"Yeah," he said softly. "And I'm lucky for it. Luckier than anyone I knew back in L.A.... and luckier, even, than a lot of people right here. Sometimes I think, why me? Why not them?"

There was something in his tone that made the hairs in the back of my neck tingle. "What d'you mean?"

"You know what I mean."

"No I don't."

"Forget it."

"You meant something by that."

"What?"

"You know what—what you said about other people here, and being lucky—"

"Forget it! What're you pushing for? It's nothing. I mean it."

"You were talking about Buzz, weren't you? That's why you brought him out."

The car lurched again, more violently this time. The engine roared, and I was very thankful the roads were deserted this time of morning, because he wasn't paying any attention to the speed. "You're mad I brought him," he said.

I got mad even just thinking about it. "He doesn't belong where we are."

58

"Why not?"

"He...Look, you know he doesn't! Don't play dumb."

"He's human."

"Not my type of human."

"Then you're as carbon-copy as the rest of them."

A hot retort jumped in my throat. But at the last second I caught it, suddenly seeing the fight looming up in front of us, and not wanting it. Buck was my buddy, my brother. What he needed now was a little advice, not blind yelling. "Look, Buck," I said, trying not to sound condescending. "You don't understand how it is. You really don't. Everybody likes you.... They like you a lot. But you're gonna make a lot of enemies if you try stuff like that with Buzz.... C'mon. I know what you meant...great idea, okay?...But it won't work. Believe me. You'll lose the crowd. Now listen. Don't blow it, okay? If you don't do it for you, then do it for me." I tried to lighten up. "Think of the dirt I'll have to take if you go wrong."

He didn't answer to that. He was silent a long time. Gradually our speed dropped down to the legal limit. "All right," he said finally. "I see you."

"Good for you." Suddenly, I was nothing but exhausted. I wanted to sleep in a bad way. I said, "Can't you get us back a little faster?"

He laughed and let the engine roar.

59

Chapter 6

I woke up at about six-thirty the next morning like I do every day of my life no matter how tired I am. Not because I set an alarm or anything, but because there's some kind of inner clock in me. The only thing that messes it up is Daylight Savings—or if I'm really sick, like that one time I drank myself blind.

Buck was still asleep. He was what he called a "night boy," and he would sleep till noon every day if he got the chance. A lot of the time I would wake him up when I woke up just to get a rise out of him, but today I decided it would be a good idea to leave him alone.

But just after I pulled on a pair of sweats and got up to go downstairs and find something to eat, he propped himself up on an elbow—scaring the heck out of me because I hadn't expected it—and ran a hand through that wispy, tawny hair of his and said, "Still mad about Buzz?"

I stared for a few seconds. His sitting up like

that had unbalanced me. "Huh? Why would I still be mad?"

His shoulders jerked up in a shrug. "Don't know. It was a dumb thing, doing it like that."

"Uh . . . yeah. Well . . . we're done with it, aren't we?"

"Hey Rich—"

I turned from the door again. "What?"

"You think anyone will make trouble with me over it?"

I looked and looked at him, looked hard into those golden brown eyes. Why would he say something like that? Had I worried him that much? "C'mon. No. Everyone likes you, and you know it. If they didn't do anything then, they won't do anything now."

"You sure?"

Solemnly, I said, "No . . . they'll hang you at dawn." Then I grinned.

Buck laughed and fell back onto the mattress and pulled a blanket over his head. His voice came from beneath it all muffled and distorted. "I'm going back to sleep."

"You're up now. Get up and keep me company. C'mon."

"I'm tiii-red, man," he moaned melodramatically.

I knew better than to argue. He'd assured himself, and now he was going to sleep in. "Fine," I said. "Sweet dreams."

"Mmm," was the only reaction I got.

I closed the door behind me and went down to the kitchen to have my solitary breakfast. Nobody but me got up early on weekends. Even Christy didn't get up until eight or nine or so to watch cartoons.

I sat there drinking orange juice and nibbling at a handful of dry Cheerios and watching the green digital numbers on the clock display on the microwave change and wondering where that vague uncomfortable chilly feeling was coming from.

By Monday, news of Buzz's appearance in major jock territory was all over. But when fingers pointed at Buck, Buck subtly pointed to Tony's approval—after all, Tony could have kicked Buzz out if that's what everyone had wanted. At least that's what Buck hinted—so when the gossip fire calmed down, Buck was in the clear and Tony was the dubious one.

I had my part in it. I'd seen how concerned Buck was, and I supported him up and down, and finally even Tony was half-convinced that Buck had had nothing to do with the scandal. I rode a high wave at the time; I loved being able to help the cool and self-possessed Buck, and I loved how everyone believed me. Pretty soon, I believed it myself.

When the talk died down, replaced with newer, hotter stuff, Tony seemed his arrogant self again and Buck was just another jock in a big crowd of jocks. He was accepted and absorbed and he wasn't any different from anyone else.

But there were hints of change.

First off, Buck's attitude toward Tony was still not as respectful as it should have been. Sure, he went along with Tony and was almost too careful never to blatantly cross him, but there was always an undercurrent of . . . What? Call it disregard, call it mockery, call it hate. Call it whatever you want, but it was there and it was there all the time.

I saw it, but I didn't want to, so I ignored it and tried to forget about it. That's the way it goes with things you don't want to know. You protect yourself by forgetting.

Tony felt it. I know he did. He felt it from the

start, and it showed in the wary look he sometimes shot Buck and it showed in the way he sometimes gave in to Buck. Buck never let that undercurrent surface, so Tony couldn't pick it out and react to it. He couldn't find it and couldn't fight it and couldn't understand it. So he chased his tail in circles and did his best to keep face.

In the second week of October, Tina Pierce decided to have a party, a party she called her "anniversary celebration." She was hand-in-hand with Tony when she came up to Buck and me in the hall, said hi to us and Kip and Jack who were with us, and invited us to her party.

Smiling cool and golden, Buck hooked the chain with Tina's ring that hung around Tony's neck with one finger and said, casually toying with it, "You've just got this big guy leashed up for life, don't you, Tina? How do you do it?"

I cringed at that; Tony's eyes were storms. But evidently Tina was really amused, because she giggled and clutched Tony's arm and said, "Wouldn't you like to know?" Tony looked ready to kill from the humiliation, but his china doll was happy with Buck's attention, and that kept him still. There was nothing he could take offense at without being considered a jealous jerk or something. That's how it always was with Buck and Tony.

Buzz McKinney was another hint of change. In spite of my warning, Buck made friends with Buzz. That never should've happened. In the first place, Buzz didn't make friends with anybody. Joe Parriot was the closest thing Buzz had to a friend, and Joe was more like a slinky loyal kind of guard dog. And in the second place, Buck was a jock and Buzz despised jocks. But Buck had a friendly relationship with Buzz, and the friendship seemed mutual.

64

One day on my way to class—I was late, actually, and the halls were pretty empty—I was caught up short when I saw Buzz and Buck leaning against the wall by a fountain, laughing and talking in low voices. Forgetting all about class, I drew up close, and when Buck saw me—his back was partly to me, so I was almost on him before he saw me—he locked eyes with me, and his eyes were flat and closed. Buzz stared blank and green at me. It wasn't hostility he projected, but an icy disinterest that was worse. I felt like I'd stumbled into a secret meeting or something. Neither of them wanted me there: I was an intruder, a jock intruder.

"Uh," I said, staring hard at Buck, "going to class?"

His eyes opened then. I could see inside again. But there was still a certain reserve in them, as if something was close to the surface that I couldn't be a part of. "Yeah," he said. "Just a minute, okay?" And he turned his back to me to say, "See ya around," to Buzz.

"What was that for?" I demanded as soon as Buzz had slunk out of earshot.

Buck knew exactly what I meant. He didn't pretend not to. "He's human," he said, looking straight at me. "I told you that before."

I couldn't say anything to that. He'd just made me feel about an inch high, like I couldn't find it in me to be understanding and he could. And maybe I couldn't. It wasn't my fault I'd never had to push for a living. That didn't make me a snobbish outsider. Still—I couldn't say anything to that. This was a side of Buck I didn't know how to deal with. So I ignored it.

Another hint of change was the romance between Joe Parriot and Steph Allen. There shouldn't have been anything too strange about that—they were two-of-a-kind sleazes—except that it was a burnout-jockette romance...brought about by Buck Dawson, thank you. And that romance led to a big mix between the two most opposed groups of high school society.

Joe's buddies started showing up in established jock places. They came with him, and he was nominally welcome as Steph's guy. Steph's jockette girlfriends—and their jock boyfriends—started hanging out with burnout types. Steph was a partyer. Burnout or jock, it didn't matter to her, so long as she had beer.

Jock was still jock. Burnout was still burnout. The thing is, people started not to care so much.

All this was fine and good. This mixing of the social groups probably should have been happening all along. Everybody—generally—was friendly and things were fine, on the surface, anyway. The number of fights went way down. Even teachers noticed the change.

Like I said, all this was fine and good...except for one thing. It was happening for all the wrong reasons. It wasn't happening because of a sudden acceptance of people's differences. It wasn't happening because of any new maturity or because everyone suddenly realized you shouldn't judge a book by its cover.

It happened because it was manipulated. And it was manipulated for a single purpose.

Buck's purpose.

Buck was accepted. He wasn't personally upsetting any balances or raising any eyebrows. Everybody loved him, no one questioned him. All he had to do to make his word law was talk to a few friends. "Hey, Buzz, mind finding something out for me?..." "Hey, Kip, you know about Jay? He's been seeing someone behind Tracy's back.

66

Someone should let her know...." "Hey, what do you know about that lit test, Joe?" And so on.

Buck could make or break a person. I actually heard him use this particular line quite a few times—and it worked every time: "I mean, don't let my opinion influence you or anything," he would say, grinning that vulnerable grin, "but I honestly think so-and-so's a real..." And then he would go on and give specific reasons why so-and-so was whatever he or she was, and in two minutes flat he would have everyone convinced.

None of it touched me, though. I was Buck's buddy, his brother. I was the one that people came to if they wanted to get in with him. I was the one Buck came to when he wasn't sure of himself. It was a good feeling. Buck had power, and the bond gave me a kind of power over him.

I remember Tony approaching me once or twice, approaching me subdued and confused, to ask me what was going on. Everything he had and everything he was was slipping away, and he was desperate to hold on. He came to me and asked me to talk to Buck, find out what he wanted, stop what was happening. Not in those words, of course, but that's what he asked for.

Tony's status as king of the jocks depended completely on the order of high school society. There had to be a ruling group, and there had to be other groups to compare it to.

Buck subverted all that. He blurred the distinctions between the groups. He mocked Tony, blunted his edge. And he made Tony's friends his friends. He stripped Tony of every advantage he'd ever had.

Tony felt this. But there was nothing he could do about it. He was forced to sit back and watch. Finally he downed enough pride to ask my help. But even though I was receptive enough and concerned because he was my friend, all I really did was ignore him. I could afford to ignore him, so I did.

I ignored him and everything else.

If I hadn't turned the other cheek like that, what happened that weekend in the middle of November might never have happened.

The middle of November is the end of fall, the beginning of winter. The leaves are long gone from the trees, and everything is brown and gray and dry and frigid.

Balancing off the coldness and bleakness and dryness is the promise of the holidays. Christmas displays are up in the department stores, and the shopping rush starts into full swing. Thanksgiving is close, and you think about what to buy your family and friends this year for Christmas. You start thinking about the looming New Year, and you think of the parties and lights and wish the last year hadn't rushed by so fast because there's still so much you want to do.

In school you think less and less about grades and more and more about vacation and partying and how you're going to spend the money Santa leaves you. College acceptances and other info flood the senior mailboxes.

Football season was finished, and wrestling—my sport—and basketball wouldn't start until December. So there was a lull in the jock world. Nobody had any schedules to follow or meets to go to. So we were all free, waiting with time on our hands and not much to do with it except cruise and drink.

That's what the middle of November is like. Brown and crisp and transitional.

A bunch of us had just sort of collected one Saturday night in an old lot right next to the high school. Of all the places we could've gone, we picked a place as close as we could get to the school we supposedly hated.

It was one of those mixed groups that were more and more the thing lately. Joe Parriot and Steph Allen were curled in the backseat of her Trans-Am. Buzz drifted somewhere in the background, and Buck and Rex and the three stooges—Jack, Mike, Trace—knotted around Rex's car along with a burnout named Carl who was tall and skinny and not too bad on the court once he got the chance to warm up. Tony brooded on the pavement a little ways apart, and I kept him company along with Bob Cordero. The usual detachment of Steph's friends hung around, and mixed with them were a couple of burnout girls. They all seemed pretty chummy.

Nobody brought any booze. Buck had confided to me that Buzz refused to come up with any more free beer, and the jocks were hoarding their money with the holidays in mind.

So there wasn't much to do. It's a shame that that's the way it was, that we couldn't have a good time without something to drink. Everybody kind of slumped around not knowing what to do. That's what happens when you depend on something like that. All the fun is taken from everything else.

To tell the truth, I didn't mind not drinking, not at all. I enjoyed the night for itself. It was frosty cold, but I had on my heavy varsity jacket with a couple of layers of sweats underneath, so I was all right. I liked the cold, as a matter of fact. It cleared my mind. Energized me, I guess. Braced me. I felt extra-alive.

And being alive that way put me in a really good mood. I felt great. I don't know. All I can say is that my blood pounded and the skin across my cheekbones was tight and cold and I was very alive.

Buck and Rex and Carl and the three stooges ambled over in a group to me and Tony and Bob, and it was a quiet, amiable type of thing. Rapport, good rapport, flowed among us, and I knew it was because it was cold and it was November and we were huddled there in camaraderie against the cold.

Then Buck opened his mouth.

His words clouded gray against the sharp blue-black sky. "Hey, Marinelli," he said softly, voice pointedly blithe and conversational. "You feeling antisocial tonight, or what? You're sitting there like you lost your best friend. . . . Liven up a little. Forget your troubles. Talk a little. C'mon. What's wrong? C'mon, Marinelli, we're all adults here. What's with you?"

Buck was goading him. It was plain as day. But then I looked at the rest of the group—Rex, Jack, Mike—and they hadn't seen a thing. So I closed my eyes to what I saw and figured maybe I was wrong.

Tony had been sitting with his arms wrapped around his knees and his chin on his arms like some kind of little kid. But now he crouched forward and shot Buck a baleful glare. He stared like that a full minute, maybe, the cold air tense and silent, before spitting out, "Lay off my back, Dawson."

He'd had it. He was tired of being pushed to the side and he knew if he didn't do something quick he'd lose it forever. So he laid a challenge.

The rapport snapped but didn't disappear. It transformed. It was something different now. Something tougher, wilder, baser, and Tony wasn't included. It was against him, and I was part of it without even knowing it.

This new rapport was something like the rapport of a crowd at a boxing match, waiting for one of the guys to fall. Or the rapport of a pack of wolves watching the pack leader rip into a rival.

Buck's face was a picture of righteous indignation. "What're you so tight about? I just asked a normal question, y'know. What's the matter? Girlfriend leave you cold or something?"

It just so happened Tony had had a bad fight with Tina that day, a yelling type of fight, right in the middle of the hall. Tina had gotten mad when Tony had tried to tell her she couldn't go to a party because he couldn't take her, and he didn't want her anywhere where he couldn't keep an eye on her. There was no way Buck couldn't have known about it, because the whole school knew about everything that happened between Tina and Tony. Buck was out for Tony and he was setting it up oh-so-perfect, and I should've tried to stop it but didn't.

That remark about Tina was all it took to make a nerve-racked, short-tempered Tony spring up from the ground and go for Buck like he meant to kill him. Lucky for Buck—I say that because Tony was more than a match for Buck and probably could've decked him with one good swing— Rex grabbed Tony by both shoulders and hauled back with all he had, keeping him from getting to Buck.

Naturally, Tony didn't appreciate that. He shook himself away, in the process giving Rex a good bruise in his recently healed face with an elbow. By that time Buck was a good fifteen feet away, flanked by Buzz and Joe on the right and Jack and Mike and Trace on the left. Rex and Bob and I stood apart, Rex rubbing his face and me praying nothing else would happen.

Buck was mad now—or at least he *looked* mad

71

"What'd you let him do that to you for?" he shouted to Rex. "He always treat you like that? You let him do that to you?"

Rex looked sideways at Tony. Chills ran down my back. Buck shouldn't have said that. He should've been concerned with his own skin. Something wasn't right.

Rex's eyes dropped. He mumbled, "It was an accident."

"Sure," scoffed Buck. "It's always an accident. Marinelli gets upset, and who does he take it out on? Everyone but himself. How many times has he kicked you when he's down? Huh, Rex buddy? How many times?"

I watched the force of those words tear at Rex. They were truth—twisted truth, sure—but still truth. Something in me hated Buck then. And something stronger shoved that hate down.

Rex stood frozen. And then he did the only thing he could. He ran. He raced for his car and threw himself into it and tore out of the lot with a squeal of tires that cut the night. A hot smell of exhaust hung in the air, and I wanted badly to run.

Tony stared blankly after Rex, dark eyes hollow, stricken. What was happening was way out of his control. It was in Buck's.

And Buck didn't ease off for a second. "Truth hurts, doesn't it, Marinelli," he taunted, moving a little closer. "Rex is too good a guy to hurt you with the truth, so he took off...."

I think Buck had more to say, but he didn't have the chance to say it because Tony went for him again. Buck didn't flinch, didn't make a move to avoid the fist that slammed into his jaw and knocked him to his knees.

And he did that on purpose. He did it on purpose because he knew exactly what would happen.

Even as I sprinted over in a useless attempt to

get between the two of them, Tony got jumped not only by Buzz and Joe but also by Jack and Mike and Trace. Tony may actually have been able to defend himself against two or three guys, but he sure couldn't fight off five. They pulled him down and pinned him on the pavement and attacked him. Joe Parriot's blade flashed in his hand.

Shock gripped me cold when I saw that. Tony could die here. I grabbed Parriot's neck and threw him harder than I've ever thrown anyone in any match and kicked his wrist to make the knife spin clear across the lot. "You'll kill him!" I screamed hoarsely. "Stop it! You'll kill him!"

I stood cold and shaking, staring as Jack and Mike and Trace backed off, nervously licking their lips and staring at their feet. Then they turned their backs and went to Buck.

Buzz shook off Bob Cordero and walked calm and smiling to Parriot, helping his guard dog up and laughing as he did.

Night-lights at the school washed dimly across the lot. Tony was a bloody mess slumped motionless on the blacktop. Unbelievably, though, he wasn't unconscious, because he kept moaning, "I thought you guys were my friends."

I wanted to cry for him. I didn't look at Buck; I couldn't. All I could do was force out the words, "Find your own way home." Then I went to Tony.

He was in awful shape. Blood masked a mass of bruises and his nose looked broken and both eyes were swollen shut and his mouth was all cut up. And that was just his face.

Bob Cordero helped me carry his deadweight past a bunch of ogling girls to my car, and he sat in the backseat with Tony while I drove to the hospital. I drove hard and fast, afraid of some kind of serious internal injury. Tony couldn't move and couldn't talk coherently, and there was blood all over.

It turned out that the only thing wrong was three cracked ribs and a lot of bad bruises and little cuts, but I spent three long hours in the county hospital's waiting room with Bob before we found that out. By that time, Tony's dad had finally shown up, looking haggard and pale and slightly drunk. But he was an okay guy; he thanked me and Bob about a thousand times before we finally got out of there.

I dropped Bob off with a few thanks of my own and headed for home. The lights were on in the house when I pulled in the driveway: Mom and Dad and Buck were waiting up. I'd called my parents from the hospital and told them everything they needed to know—which was that Tony got hurt bad and I'd had to rush him to the hospital and no it wasn't necessary for them to come out, I was fine.

"How is he?" Mom wanted to know as soon as I was in the door.

"All right," I said shortly. I caught the confused hurt look on her face, so I amended, "They were cleaning him up when I left. They didn't find anything real serious...couple broken ribs, maybe...." I couldn't help looking at Buck then.

I was almost sorry I did. I'd been building up a beautiful fury; I'd been ready to chew him to pieces. But I looked at him with his bruised jaw and saw how drawn and tired and worried sick he was. And those emotions weren't an act. They were real. They were there.

"I'd rather just get to sleep," I told my parents. Again there was that confused look, but they nodded, so I dragged myself upstairs and into my room. I didn't bother to undress or anything. I just sat on my bed and waited for Buck.

My wait was short. A half-minute later he slipped in, pushing the door softly shut. "What happened wasn't my fault," he said, looking at the floor.

"Sure." The word was flat, sarcastic.

Buck looked at me, and those golden brown eyes were pained and pleading. "It wasn't my fault," he said again. "I didn't know they'd go after him like that. You can't say what they did was my fault."

At least he wasn't denying his own part in it. Maybe he knew better than to deny it. I absorbed what he said without comment and studied the blue glass stone in my class ring.

He took my silence as an accusation. "It wasn't my fault," he pleaded once more. "He brought it on himself with how he acted.... I didn't do anything. It wasn't my fault. Listen, Rich. He just got beat up. That's all. It's not that bad. I've been messed up worse in my time...." He trailed off, hesitant, unsure, and then decided to pick up where he'd left off. "Don't be mad at me, Rich. I didn't do anything. Nothing happened to him that hasn't happened to any other guy. I'm sure he's done his fair share of jumping.... He would've jumped me. It's not like he's any different...."

I kept absorbing and I kept studying my ring. "Tell that to Tony."

He pulled at the long hair in back of his neck, chewed on his lip. "What do you want me to do about it, Rich? What? There's nothing I can do."

"Right."

"C'mon! What? I can't change what happened."

I tugged at my high-tops, lips tight. "Too bad, isn't it? Bet you're real upset."

His eyes were wide, apprehensive. "That's not right."

"Neither was what happened."

"It wasn't my fault? I didn't lay a finger on him, dammit!" His voice was urgent, nervous. "You know I didn't touch him. C'mon, Rich! How can you blame me if I didn't even touch him? I didn't do anything!"

"Sure."

"Rich ... C'mon. Please. Don't do this to me."

What did he want? What did he expect? Did he want me to just forget all about it? Things weren't that simple. "Don't do what?" I said. "Don't be mad at what happened to my friend? What you *made* happen? Sorry, Dawson. I don't buy it."

His eyes lowered. "All right. Okay. What do you want me to do about it, then?"

The question caught me short. I looked sharp at him. "There's nothing you can do."

Quietly he said, "Then don't cut me up for it anymore. You're cutting me up, and it's not doing anything except mess us up."

My throat tightened. What could I say to that? I was cutting him up, it was messing things up, and it wasn't doing anything for Tony. And there was something pathetic, and ego-building, about the way the super-controlled Buck was pleading for my acceptance, my forgiveness. Buck, who acted like he didn't need anyone most of the time, needed me. I pulled my sweats over my head and rolled onto my side to face a wall. "Just shut up about it. Leave me alone. I'm tired. I don't want to talk about it."

"It's over, then."

I didn't want to have to think about an answer to that. So I mashed a pillow over my head and didn't say anything.

Chapter 7

News of Tony's getting jumped spread like wild-fire. The gossip lines hummed, and by Monday morning everybody knew every detail of what had happened. By Monday morning everybody knew Tony had been put down.

He had to run the gauntlet. He'd been taken down and he made no effort to get back up. He'd lost and he was ashamed and he wanted to be left alone with his shame. His pride had been cut to the quick, and he didn't want anyone gawking at the wound. He shut everybody out—Tina broke up with him by third period, throwing his ring in his face—and refused to talk to anyone except Bob Cordero or me. And what he said to Bob or me wasn't much—only the barest, thinnest necessities.

Sixth-period study hall that Monday was a tense, awful forty-five minutes. Tony walked in stiff and slow and fierce, head angled low to avoid meeting any of the curious glances of the socials and the jocks and the mocking glances of the burnouts. He sat down just as slow and stiff—his ribs were taped and you could tell they hurt even though he never would have admitted it—and gave me a brief acknowledgment by making eye contact before opening up some book with a deliberateness that was as plain as a Do Not Disturb sign.

Buck came in, and things got worse. He wasn't stupid enough to try to make an apology, but I could see the apology in his face and I didn't like it because it was much too late for it. So Buck sat down in his seat behind Tony and exchanged a few phrases with his jock friends and his burnout friends and with me and then was silent.

I glanced to Tony. He was hunched over his book and scribbling something in a notebook. Buck gnawed his lip. Finally he leaned forward and said in a low voice, "I'm sorry about your ribs, Marinelli."

Tony's pen stopped mid-scribble. He just sat there and stared at his book through those bruised dark eyes of his. I thought I saw his hands tremble. Just when it seemed like he couldn't stare like that a second longer, he shook his head once and said without turning around, "No you aren't, Dawson. You aren't sorry at all."

And then he hunched even deeper and started scribbling again.

A dry, breathy rasp came from Buck's throat. Tight-lipped and hard-eyed, he leaned back in his seat, his stare never leaving Tony's bent shoulders. Almost inaudibly he mumbled, "I better not ever hear you say I didn't try, Marinelli."

I looked down at my desk and wished I hadn't heard that mumble.

* * *

Not long after the big fight, something happened to me that took me out of circulation in jock society for a while. This something had my full attention, and I didn't have the time to notice what was going on around me.

What this something was is that I fell in love with Katy Avendell.

Katy was in my first-period trig class and my seventh-period English class, and in both classes we ended up sitting next to each other because of the way the seating chart read. She was an outgoing but soft-spoken social—definitely not one of the airheads—whom I'd known since she moved to our district in ninth grade. She and I got along pretty well—more than pretty well. We were better friends than I realized for a long time. She was easy to talk to, and an easy talker in return. We never had any awkward places in our conversations, and she was one girl I never flirted with. I didn't have to. She was the kind of girl you didn't play stupid games with.

Katy was warm and earthy and carefree, without being transparent or bubbly, and she was beautiful inside and out. Even now I miss her so much that I hurt.

I might never have had the chance to miss her if it weren't for Don Pressman, fastest mover in the jock crowd.

It's weird. He wasn't that good-looking and his personality wasn't the greatest, but he had girls following him in herds. And he never discouraged any of them.

Don and I had the same lunch—we sat across from each other. We also had the same class right before lunch in a room right by the cafeteria, so we always got there before everyone else. Anyway, this one day in the middle of November—right after Tony got jumped—Don said to me between wolfing down his hamburger and engulfing his French fries, "Wanna go out on Friday?"

"Out where?" I said.

"Movie or something. I told Laurie I'd take her out."

"Why don't you take her out by yourself?"

Don swallowed the remains of his lunch. "Don't you want to go out?" he countered. "Want your French fries?"

I dumped the fries on his plate. "They're yours," I said.

I don't like them too well. I don't like pizza or hot dogs too much, either. I guess I'm just an abnormal American youth.

Don took time out to clean up my fries. By that time the rest of the jocks who sat at our table had appeared, and Don scouted for stray food before saying in my direction, "Don't you?"

"Don't I what?"

"Want to go out?"

"I don't know. I guess...."

"Then you can pick me and Laurie up around seven."

I couldn't help smiling. "Wait a minute," I said. "Are you telling me I'm the wheels for your date? Hey, Don, you know what 'tacky' means? How about 'stupid'? Or try, 'No way'?"

"You'll have someone, too," explained Don. He leaned forward. "See, I *told* Laurie...and I can't get the car.... C'mon, Candyman. Please?"

There's something about Don—probably the same something that attracts all those girls—that makes it almost impossible to refuse him. And I really didn't have anything against going out. I had money and I knew I could have the car Friday night and I didn't have any other plans. So I smiled and called Don a few affectionate dirty names and said, "Oh, okay, I guess. But you better set me up with someone good."

He looked at me with wide eyes. "Who said I was going to set you up? Don't you got anyone you want to ask?"

I shrugged. "Not particularly. Should I?"

Don shrugged too. "Nooo," he said. "But there's gotta be someone."

"Nope. No one."

"What about Debbie?" he said, remembering how the two of us had played the game.

"Spare me," I groaned. "She's so dumb it drives me crazy." And that was the truth.

"You'd have a good time."

"No, I wouldn't. Believe me, I wouldn't."

"What about Katy Avendell?"

"What?" I looked at him like he was crazy. It was like his asking me to ask out my own sister. "I can't."

"Why not?" he wanted to know.

I squirmed at that one. I'd suddenly realized I didn't have an answer. "Just because," I said.

"Why don't you ask her? There's nothing wrong with her, is there? You talk to her all the time. And she knows Colleen," he said, referring to the social girl whose attention I'd tried to attract for a year—the same Colleen who'd called Buck that first day of school. Don mentioned Colleen because in high school society it's important to know who a person's friends are.

Not that Colleen's name influenced my decision. The more I thought about Katy, really thought about her, the more she seemed like a good choice. I'd have a good enough time and I'd have someone I could talk to without putting on an act and I wouldn't have to play the game, which would be a real relief. I'd had enough of it to last me a lifetime.

I said to Don, "She sounds good, I guess. I'll let you know what's up by tomorrow."

So I guess you can say it was Don Pressman's fault that I fell in love and forgot about everything for a while.

I wonder if I ever thanked him for it.

Seventh period rolled around, and that's when I asked Katy if she wanted to go out with me and Don Pressman and his girlfriend on Friday night. It was an easy thing to do. But that was how the whole relationship was. Easy and comfortable.

I remember saying to her just before the bell signaling the beginning of class rang, "I mean, don't get the wrong idea or anything. I'm just asking because I know we'll have fun."

She laughed when I said that, and I laughed too. But I was more right than I knew, because I had more than a fun time. I fell in love.

That Friday I picked Katy up first, then Don and Laurie. Katy and Laurie knew each other and they got along fine, and naturally Don and I got along well, so it started out right.

Once we got to the theater, it was even better. We took four seats across—with me and Don next to each other in the middle and Katy and Laurie on either side. But as soon as the show started, Don may as well not have existed. Katy started laughing—it was a comedy—and making comments, and I laughed too because what she said was funny. Pretty soon, we were throwing these comments back and forth almost faster than we could talk. Like I said, I felt easy with her. I didn't have to act. That was just the way she was.

After a while Don and I went out and brought back Cokes and popcorn. It was at that little lull after we'd sat back down that I looked over at Katy chewing on the straw of her Coke and realized

I'll bet I looked shocked. I know I felt shocked. "Do you want me to?" I said stupidly. *How to Act Like an Idiot,* by Rich Candy.

"Yeah," she said simply.

So I did.

And I left Katy Avendell's house knowing I was in love.

That Saturday was a good day, mostly because it followed Friday.

Buck got up around eleven, but only because I made him. He'd stayed home the night before—the outside partying had slacked off with the cold and the loss of a jock king—so I figured he'd had plenty of rest.

I woke him by setting my Walkman beside his ear and turning it up full-blast. He jumped high, all right, and then he almost hit me before he fully awoke. I guess it was kind of sadistic to pull something like that, but I couldn't help myself. It was a habit left over from the days when Bill and I shared the room. Bill used to like to sleep in too, and I had a thousand and one cruel and unusual ways to get him up.

I never said Bill and I were examples of brotherly love.

Anyway, I made Buck get up; after the initial shock wore off, he was fine. "So how'd it go?" he wanted to know right away.

I shrugged. "It was good."

Buck grinned at me. "How good?"

I thought about that a minute. It was a question I really couldn't answer in words. How could I describe to Buck what I couldn't describe to myself? All I knew was that at the moment everything looked good.

Finally, I said, "I'm calling her today." It was all I said, but Buck understood.

He caught me in an elbow lock around the throat. "Good luck," he said, pulling me back down. Being rough like that was his way of showing... well, affection. It was the only way he showed it. Not that most guys aren't that way—they rough each other up where girls would be hugging each other—but Buck showed it that way because it was the only way he felt safe with. He'd grown up learning that letting people know you cared was letting people have a way to hurt you, and it was a lesson he couldn't shake. So he never showed any affection except through playing rough.

I took him up on his move and we wrestled for a minute or so before I had him down and pinned. I grinned at him. "Don't forget I can still take you down, Buck-boy." I held him a few seconds more just to enjoy the winning.

He squirmed free as soon as I eased off. He laughed and said, "You were just lucky."

"That's what you think," I said.

I called Katy sometime in the early afternoon. I wanted to find out if she was busy.

It turned out she was just about to walk out the door to go shopping with a friend. But we had a short warm talk, and she promised to call me when she got home, so I was happy and hung up the phone with a smile on my face.

Buck had been slinking in and out of the room as I talked, and every time he came in he gave me the same big cocky grin. Under other circumstances, I might've been ticked off by that kind of thing, but I was in too high a mood to think bad of anything.

When I hung up, Buck was right there. "So what's up?" he said.

"I d'know," I said. "She's going out."

Buck raised an eyebrow.

"Shopping," I added.

"She's a nice girl," he said. "A nice type."

"I'm glad you approve," I said, just a little dryly. "I mean, otherwise, forget it."

He pointed. "I know what I'm talking about, Rich," he informed me. "Believe me, I've seen a lot of types, and she's a nice one."

He sure wasn't exaggerating when he said he'd seen a lot of types. Buck had been a big hit with the female population of the school, and he'd attracted them from every group. He'd had that call from Colleen, prima donna of the socials, on the first day of school; from there, his luck had never stopped running.

The jockettes, the social girls, the burnout girls, even the brainy girls all went for Buck. He did everything he could to make each and every girl feel that she was his favorite.

"We're just really close friends," you'd hear some girl say about him. "It's almost like we're brother and sister...." And you'd know they'd rather be much more than brother and sister.

The funny thing was, Buck never had anything more than a brief, low-key interest in any of them. No one girl caught his eye for very long. He would pay extra attention to a particular girl for a few days, sometimes; maybe show up at her house or even pair off with her for a short time. But that was it. He would back off and ease out before anything real started, and his technique was close to perfect. It was rare, very rare, that a girl would be upset or feel dumped or used by him.

Buck, the man with the friendly golden charm.

I think he was afraid of girls, to tell the truth. He didn't know how to handle an in-depth relationship, so he shied away from any chance of one. But at the same time he loved the attention and loved girls for what they could give him on a superficial level, so he kept them near him without letting them get close to him.

So even if Buck's remark about knowing a lot of types was arrogant, it was true. And I wasn't about to make an issue of it. So I just agreed with him. "She is nice," I said.

Casually, he said, "You think it'll get somewhere?"

"I hope so," I said.

And I meant it.

Chapter 8

Katy and I became an item.

We were a pair. We were seen together all the time in the halls in school, and we were seen together all the time out of school too. We saw a lot of each other, as a matter of fact, and neither of us was seeing anyone else.

Not that one of us couldn't have gone out with someone else if one of us had wanted to. We were just too interested in each other.

We never officially "went" with each other, though. To be honest, it was unnecessary. We had a close relationship and we didn't need each other's class rings to make that relationship solid and real. We had each other, plain and simple, and that was enough.

Our time together was always low-key, easy. We never stopped being friends, and I think that's one of the things that made it so good. Even after we'd been together for weeks, I'd still hear about people asking, "Do they like each other?" Like I said, we were low-key. We saved our personal affection for when we were alone, unlike a lot of couples, especially the junior and sophomore kids. You'd see some pretty heavy stuff against the lockers and outside the doors. It was supposedly against the rules to indulge in that kind of thing, but it was a rule nobody paid attention to.

I can't say I'm completely guiltless of that stuff myself, but I always managed to keep my passion under control. Not to mention that I did outgrow it—*it* meaning the love-in-the-halls stuff—by the time my senior year rolled around.

Anyway, Katy and I behaved ourselves and behaved ourselves so well that some people didn't even realize we were a couple.

And that's the way we liked it.

We shared a lot of good times. Some of the best of those times were when we just spent time at home, her home or mine, doing little things. We played cards with Christy, listened to the radio, helped her mom and dad create some monster health food dinner, watched the snow fall, played with Tom, the ex-stray tomcat who'd joined our family, and talked and laughed and held hands.

When we were alone, she was very sexy, and so was I. Kissing someone you care about is a thousand worlds away from kissing someone just to satisfy a sex urge, and that's all I'm going to say about it.

Sort of like the romance between Steph Allen and Joe Parriot bringing the jocks and the burnouts together, the romance between Katy and me pulled me away from the jock world and close to the social's. Katy was involved in quite a few of those clubs and things, and she got me involved too. After a little initial resistance, I thought it was fun. Katy's friends leaned more toward the responsible end of the social spectrum; most of them were themselves, and I liked the idea of being myself.

Sure, there were some of those social types I really couldn't stand, but there are going to be people you don't like and people who don't like you everywhere you go. I just stayed away from the ones who bothered me and enjoyed the rest.

I took Katy with me to a couple of jock parties, but she wasn't that interested. She didn't go for drinking just to blow your mind. I'd never been really interested in that kind of thing myself—I'd always just gone along with the crowd—so it was easy for her to convince me that the drinking wasn't that much fun.

The last major jock party I went to with her was in the second weekend of December. It was at Jack Sempsey's house, and Jack's dad was laughably tolerant of the idea of a bunch of Jack's friends drinking themselves crazy in his basement.

The usual crowd was there with the usual extras in the form of girlfriends and boyfriends and buddies. Tony was conspicuously absent. He had a definite hate for Jack. Lately, Tony had been climbing to his feet a little, getting back into circulation, but he was nowhere in sight of where he once was. Some people sympathized with him, sure, but nobody including me did anything more than sympathize. Tony just didn't have the power he used to.

I'd been a little uneasy about taking Katy with me to Jack's place. I knew she really didn't get into that kind of gathering. I told her as much, but all she had to say was, "I'm not an angel. You don't have to carry me over mud puddles."

"You are an angel," I'd said back.

"Ever look at the tarnish on my halo?"

"There's no tarnish...."

"I like to get a little drunk every once in a while."

"Kat," I said, honestly shocked.

"Well, I do. Stop treating me like an angel."

So we were at this party at Jack's house, and it wasn't wild yet, but it was getting there. I'd drunk about four beers and Katy had had three when she leaned back—she was sitting in my lap—and whispered, "Let's go, Rich. I'm bored of watching *Sink the Titanic*."

Sink the Titanic is a game where the idea is to take turns filling this glass floating in a big potful of beer without sinking the glass. And whoever sinks the glass has to drink all the beer in the pot. The purpose of the game is to get bombed. Kip Mason—the weird guy who'd do anything, and I mean anything, for money—loved that game.

Cute, huh?

"I'm not driving," I told her. "I don't want to wreck—"

"You told me that once already. Can't Buck take us home now?"

"He's not going to want to leave."

"He can come back after he takes us home."

"But if he comes back, he'll stay; then you'll have to stay at my house till really late, 'cause I won't have the car and Mom and Dad are out, and you'll get in trouble...."

She slid off my lap. "I'm going to ask him if he'll go now."

I watched her navigate through a crowd of girls to get to Buck. She pulled him off to the side, and I saw her smile up at him and put her hands on his shoulders. A minute later, I saw him nod, and the two of them made their way to where I was sitting.

"Let's get out of here as quiet as we can," said

Buck with a little grimace, and I knew what he meant. We caught Jack on the way out the door to say good-bye. He was awful drunk, but I think he got the idea.

So we got out without any trouble, and we were on our way home with Buck as chauffeur.

The lights were all out at the house. Mom and Dad were at a party of their own—an office party—and Bill was out carousing somewhere and Christy was staying over at her friend Missy's. So Buck and Katy and I had the place to ourselves.

We went into the den to look at the Christmas tree—it was a real one with tinsel and lights and glass bulbs and beads, which we'd just put up that morning—and to fool around with the train. Dad's a bit of a model-train buff, so we have this really elaborate set under the tree. Everything's in scale and there are all kinds of buildings and plastic people and fake little trees and all that stuff.

Buck loved the tree. He also loved the train set. I swear he spent three hours down there with my dad oiling wheels and burnishing tracks and all that other preparatory stuff no one else in the family wanted to do. As a matter of fact, Buck loved everything about Christmas. He loved the snow. He loved the lights. He found joy in everything. The littlest things, things I'd always taken for granted, like deciding what to buy the dog and cat for Christmas, were all big deals to him. He faced it all with an eagerness that was almost childish but also was very serious.

After a few minutes of looking at the tree, Buck went into the kitchen to make coffee, insisting, "It can't hurt."

I wasn't so sure about that—I'd already had to make one trip to the bathroom—but I let him have his way because it was a chance to be alone with Katy and there was no letting him not have it.

He took his time. I was sitting on the floor, and Katy leaned back against my chest and pulled my arms around her waist. The colored lights on the Christmas tree threw patterns across the carpet in the dark room, and Katy's lips were on the underside of my jaw when Buck came back with his coffee and said, "Oh, isn't this cozy. Can I join in?"

He set the mugs on an end table and knelt down behind me and gave us both a hug and a quick kiss on the cheek, which made me lift an eyebrow and seriously wonder if maybe he'd broken his no-drink rule. But it was all just part of his high holiday mood.

Still on his knees, he leaned over and latched onto a couple of the mugs and put them into my and Katy's hands. "Drink it," he urged.

I did. It had a strange rich spicy taste, one that I kept wanting a little more of. "This is good," said Katy. "What's in it?"

Buck rocked back on his heels. "Ancient Chinese secret," he said, smiling. "Some nutmeg, some cinnamon, little bit of other stuff."

"Huh," was my comment. "Think you're some kind of chef?"

Buck flashed a big grin and fell onto the couch. "Maybe," he said. "I have many hidden talents."

"Do you have a talent for disappearing?"

Katy elbowed me, hard. "Rich!"

Buck's eyes were wide. "If that's what you *want*, I can handle it...."

"No," said Katy firmly. "You stay."

"Woof woof," said Buck obediently, settling happily back into the couch.

For a minute, I wanted to kill him. But as a matter of fact, I liked it that way. I more than liked it. I was easy and warm with Katy in my arms, and I was easy knowing I was with the people I'd most want to be with.

That was a good night.

As Christmas approached, Mom went crazy. She was having three of her sisters and one of my dad's brothers and all their families over the day after Christmas—it was Mom's year to host the gathering—and the kitchen was stacked with all the food she was getting ready. Not only did she have the relatives to worry about, she also had millions of presents to take care of and visiting neighbors on Christmas Day to remember and the family's traditional turkey dinner for Christmas Eve to make.

So Mom—who really doesn't like cooking and baking much but does a great job anyway—was in a rotten mood, which got Dad in a rotten mood, which could've spread its way to Buck and me but didn't. Buck would've smiled if someone slapped him in the face, and all I had on my mind was Katy.

Christy went crazy too. She couldn't wait to see what she'd gotten for Christmas. She'd given up Santa Claus around first grade, but she definitely hadn't given up any excitement about the whole deal. She was a little sneak, too, a wonderful trade taught to her by Bill, who casually suggested the linen closet as a good place to hide toys.

I found Christy two days before Christmas buried under the sheets she'd dragged down from the third shelf.

I don't know if Bill went crazy. I didn't see much of him. He stayed locked up in his cave and made himself deaf with his stereo headphones and only came out for meals and friends and the bathroom, in that order.

Even Katy went a little crazy. She was bright-eyed and eager as a little girl. She called me up all breathless and excited on the twenty-third and begged me to take her on a last-second shopping trip. I agreed, and we went to the mall. The place was a zoo, a zoo full of insane people.

Everybody went crazy during the holidays, and it was great. That craziness only comes once a year.

Somehow Mom managed to be all settled by Christmas Eve day. We had the traditional turkey dinner in the dining room around seven, and the candles were lit and the lights were off, and the tree glowed. There was a lot of food, and for once I made Mom happy by eating what seemed like pounds of it.

I'd wanted Katy to have dinner with us, but she'd had to go to her grandparents' farm in Maine with her parents and brother, who was home from college. That sounded nice and Currier and Ives-ish and all, but I wanted her to be with me. Snow flurried outside the window, flecking white under the streetlights. The promise of a white Christmas was something I'd looked forward to; all that was missing to make the day perfect was Katy.

After dinner was finished and everything cleaned up, we all went into the den to sit around the tree. Dad turned the stereo to some soft station playing twenty-four-hour Christmas music. We sat there quiet for what seemed like a very long time. We weren't doing anything more than taking in the quiet and thinking about whatever we were thinking about, but it filled time.

Then Christy stood up, marched to the tree, threw up her arms and yawned, and then said, "Let's all go to bed so Santa Claus can come!" There was a big smile on her face. Like I said,

Christy doesn't believe in Santa Claus, but she does believe in presents—she's a material girl—and she knew that the presents wouldn't come until after she'd slept.

Everybody laughed, even Bill who liked to think he was above laughing at funny things little kids say.

"You can go to bed," said Mom, "but that doesn't mean Santa's coming any earlier."

"But if I sleep, I won't know it's not earlier," Christy pointed out.

"Very wise," said Dad seriously.

"Go ahead," said Mom. "Upstairs."

Try getting Christy into bed that early any other day of the year and see what happens.

So, anyway, Christy made her rounds, giving everybody a Christmas hug and good-night kiss, and then she bounced out of the room in a way that told me this was one eleven-year-old who was way too wound up to get to sleep in the near future.

Dad slapped his hands on his knees. "Well, boys, Edna's waiting."

That meant Mom and Dad were going to visit old Edna and her husband across the street, which left me and Bill and Buck to slouch around the house.

There really wasn't much to do. Bill turned on some holiday movie on cable and Buck fooled with the train and I sat there and snatched glances at the snow piling into layers outside the window and wondered what Katy was doing and if she was having a good time.

When the movie was over, Bill drifted up to his cave and was followed by Buck, which left me alone to brood in front of the TV and the tree. I must've fallen asleep there on the couch—I fall asleep really easy when I let my mind wander—

because next thing I knew it was a quarter to eleven and Mom and Dad were just coming in the door. They saw me there on the couch in the den and asked me to help them bring in Christy's presents from the trunk of the car.

So I helped them set up Christy's presents under the tree. After we were done, Mom shoved me up the stairs, saying, "Santa can't show while you're awake."

"Please," I said, but I went upstairs anyway and left them to themselves.

Buck was still awake, which didn't surprise me, because he was always up at night. He was mostly under the blankets, and he had headphones on. I stole a look at the volume control, and it was way up. He would go deaf if he didn't watch it.

I shrugged off my clothes and got into bed and fell asleep pretty quick, I think. The light was on, but that was something I'd gotten used to with Buck around.

Next thing I knew, Buck was shaking me, shaking me hard and saying, "Hey!" in my ear.

Now, I'm an early riser, and I don't need much sleep, and I got a kick out of waking Buck up in the mornings, but I hate it when people wake me up. I get irritated, more irritated than I should. I scowled up at him and growled, "What?"

"Come with me," he said, simple and quiet. He looked down at me, but I couldn't read anything in those golden brown eyes. That worried me. I wondered what was wrong. "Come on," he repeated. "Downstairs."

I threw back the blankets, shivering when the air hit my skin. Without a word Buck handed me a flannel shirt he'd picked up from the floor, and without a word I slid into it and folded my arms tight against me for warmth as I followed him down the steps and into the dark and silent den. He flipped the switch that turned on the Christmas-tree lights. They were almost eerie, that late at night, with snow blanketing the street.

"Sit down," he said.

I did like he told me. The lights reflected off Christy's presents, the presents I'd helped bring in earlier, red and blue and green and yellow. And still I was wondering. "Buck—"

"Shut up." He was smiling now. I could see that toothpaste-commercial smile even in the dimness of the tree lights. "Hold on. This was all planned...." He crouched down, and I was crazy with wondering what was going on.

Abruptly, he stood and tossed something at me—almost threw it at me. Luckily, I caught it before it hit me in the face.

It was a box, a plain narrow box with some kind of raised symbol on the top. I just stared at it. I didn't know what to do with it.

Buck sat there with his arms around his knees, light reflecting off his bare shoulders, darkness making him look trawnier than ever. He looked at me. "It opens, y'know."

"Oh," I said stupidly. Sure enough, it opened. And inside was a watch. A gold watch. It shone and glinted.

"Damn," I breathed. "Damn, Buck." I lifted it out and held it in the palm of my hand. It was heavy and warm and I could feel the tick of it like a tiny heartbeat. It was golden and beautiful, and it was as alive and real as the bond that surged stronger than ever between us. "Why?"

"I wanted to," he said. "That's all. I wanted to."

"This is so damn expensive...."

"All honest money."

"I wasn't—"

"I know you weren't. I just wanted you to know

that." His eyes were big and golden. "Would it have made a difference, though?"

"I'd rather have it honest," I said automatically, and I hated the quickness of it.

"That's why it is."

I snapped it on. The adjustment was perfect. "How did you—"

"Dad helped pick it out."

The word slipped so smoothly from him. *Dad.*

Suddenly, I was confused, and the confusion came from a mix of embarrassment and inability to say thank you the way I wanted to. "I don't have anything like this to give you," I said slowly. I'd gotten some tapes for him, no big deal, and I knew it would break the mood to give them to him now.

Buck sat up and drew closer, close enough to reach out and touch my knees if he'd tried. He swallowed once and looked away. "You've already give me enough," he said to the floor. "You gave me...this." His arm swept across the room. "You gave me...life, Rich. I mean that. I swear I mean it...." He was close to talking in pants, the way he had on that first day he'd told me what he'd been through.

Tangible feeling flowed between us. Without thinking, I reached down and clasped his shoulders, and he did the same back. It was a natural thing, but there was an electricity in it, an electricity that stunned me. I hadn't expected it, and I don't think Buck had, either. We stayed like that a minute there in the dimness, me on the edge of the couch, Buck on his knees on the floor.

For a split second—just a split second, only a split second—I wished I could hold him closer, wished I could show him what I felt the same way I showed Katy what I felt. After that split second I felt an awful guilt and wondered what made me think that way even for a split second; that wondering led to a kind of revulsion, which led me to wondering what something like that was really like. Buck would know what it was like....

No. No, he wouldn't. Because what Buck had known had nothing to do with love, which was what I was thinking about.

I forced myself to turn off that train of thought. I did a pretty good job of it. It was like turning off running water. To ease the tenseness, I laughed and said, "Thousands of cars in that parking lot, thousands of easy targets, and you pick mine."

He laughed very softly, and his eyes were far away, "And you just happened to be coming back...."

"And the next car just happened to pull too close, so you couldn't get out the other side...."

His hands slid from my shoulders, and he pointed at me. He seemed a little shaken and I wondered if he'd been caught by the same thing that for a split second had caught me. "It's those just-happened-to's that make all the difference," he said. "It scares me when I think about them all. They've run my life, my whole life, Rich.... They scare me. You know what I'm saying? I hate them. I don't like things....*controlling* my life."

"You rule your life," I told him. "You decide what's what. It's all up to you, Buck-boy."

He shook his head. "No," he said. "No. It's not up to me at all. Something else decides it."

I almost snarled the next word. "*No.* Nothing else."

He looked at me. "Merry Christmas."

Chapter 9

Christmas vacation was exceptionally good for more than one reason, and that made going back to school worse than it usually was.

To wrap things up, I'll give a run down on what happened the rest of vacation.

Christmas Day came and the presents were opened, and then the neighbors started coming. Buck and I got out of there pretty quick and did some visiting of our own. To let you know what an excellent mood I was in, I even asked Bill to come with us. I think he almost dropped dead when I did. He just didn't expect it. But he came with us, and the three of us ended up having a pretty good time. Bill showed us off to a few of his friends, and my buddies made a pet out of him.

I'd never thought Bill would be the type to go for being a pet, a little brother to a whole pack of guys. He was too caught up in being independent and tough. But he got along fine with my friends, a lot better than he ever got along with me, and he also showed them a lot more respect. Maybe that's why they made him a pet.

Then came December twenty-sixth. The wild day, the day of the relatives. Three of my aunts and my oldest uncle on my dad's side and all their kids. That made a total of twenty-five people, and more than half of them were under sixteen. The only cousin as old as I was my oldest aunt's oldest daughter, Sherri. Sherri is a little weird if you ask me—she's got air for a brain—but she's okay, I guess.

Anyway, we had all these relatives who stayed until two in the morning. It was a relief to see them go. I can take partying with a bunch of wild jocks, but putting up with a herd of little kids and adolescents really wore me down. I think I would've gone crazy if Buck hadn't been there to take some of the police work off my hands.

New Year's Eve I spent at Katy's house. She'd come home from Maine just a day and a half before. I'd managed to see her a couple of short times, but I didn't get the chance to really be with her until then. Mr. and Mrs. Avendell held a semi-intellectual party for some people from the office, and since Katy had to stay there and show off her smile and crush ice in the kitchen, I went over and kept her company. We stayed out of the way of the execs, drank wine and champagne—which made me feel pretty ritzy not to mention buzzed—watched the countdown on TV, and generally kept ourselves entertained.

I ended up sleeping in her brother's room, and I didn't go home until six-thirty next evening.

So that wraps up the holidays.

Like I said, going back to school after all that was a bad deal. But I survived it. I had Katy to focus my attention on, and that pulled me through.

Buck had something to keep his attention too.

He actually became more than lukewarmly interested in a particular girl, and that girl happened to be Tina, Tony's ex. They called each other, and Buck was over at her place every minute he could be there—we had some good arguments over who would get the car—and after two weeks of that they were going together. It was the first time Buck had ever gone with a girl, and if I had thought about it, I would have seen it for what it was.

To the victor go the spoils.

The only negative side of that relationship that I paid any attention to was its effect on Tony. It was pitiful how he tried to pretend he didn't give a damn about what Tina did. But it bit him to the bone and everyone knew it. I think he honestly loved that girl, and it hurt him like nothing else ever had to see her hand-in-hand with the guy who'd brought him down. There wasn't any anger involved in the hurt, just a deep, deep pain, and it was awful to see it in him. In fact, it was so awful that most people just ignored it. The fact that Tony might be sensitive inside was something nobody wanted to think about because it made them feel guilty for pushing him to the side.

I know I felt a little guilty.

But I had Katy to take my mind off guilt.

Buck and Tina broke up about two weeks after they'd started going together. It was a simple mutual deal, no fighting or tears or anything. They stayed friends, visited each other once in a while, leaned on each other for "companionship" when no one else happened to be in reach.

Buck gave me a big song and dance about how they'd decided freedom and cooling off was the best thing for both of them. Tina said the same thing.

"It's better just to be good friends," she sighed.

"I just don't *want* another in-depth relationship so soon after the *other* one. . . ."

Tina sure thought that was the way it was . . . but Buck?

He'd gotten tired of her. He didn't care. Nothing more. He didn't have any feeling for her at all. I knew that's how it really was because I knew Buck. He couldn't pull his act on me. But I didn't push him for the truth, mostly because I didn't care.

Just for the record, Tony almost broke down with relief when he found out Buck and Tina were no more.

It surprised me when two days after Buck and Tina had broken up, I came home from wrestling practice and found him talking on the phone. Not that his talking on the phone surprised me—he got a lot of calls—but he was talking to Tina. His voice was his Tina voice, low and purring, and his expression—half-smiling, sly, golden—was his Tina expression. Buck had different attitudes for different people, and this particular attitude was reserved for Tina alone. I knew that he and Tina were still friendly, but it surprised me that he was using the same girlfriend intimacy with the girl he'd just broken up with.

That's why I was even more surprised when Buck snapped his fingers at me a couple of minutes later and said, "For you." He dropped the phone on the floor by the couch and wandered away with this weird smile on his face.

I shrugged to myself and picked up the phone. "Hello?"

"Rich?"

I almost fell over. It wasn't Tina. It was Katy.

"Wait a minute," I said. "Kat . . . What were you talking to Buck for?"

"Because you weren't home," she said, saying

it like she was explaining it to me for the hundredth time.

"How long were you talking?"

"Rich!" She was shocked and mad at my tone, and I don't blame her. "What's the matter with you? We were just talking....Am I suddenly not allowed to talk to other guys?"

"Not him," I told her. I tried to make a joke out of it. "He's a lady-killer."

"For God's sake. He's your brother."

No he's not, yelled a petty little voice in my mind. But suddenly I felt rotten for talking like that. "Okay, okay, okay. You're right. I'm sorry. So whip me." She laughed, and I forgot about it.

At least until the next day.

The next day really fired up my jealousy. And the worst part of it is that there was absolutely no reason to get fired. My jealousy was stupid and irrational and baseless and I knew it, but knowing it didn't do anything to cool it.

I think one of the reasons this thing was so powerful was that on some subconscious level, I knew I'd turned my back on Tony and the way everything used to be and should have been in exchange for a little bit of petty glory—the glory of being high up in the system with Buck. Things were going better for me than they ever had before, and I was willing to give up some identity and some values to keep it that way. Or at least outwardly I was willing. Things bothered me inside, and it showed up as jealousy.

I had practice again the next day, so I wasn't home until around a quarter after five. I scuffed down the front hall to the kitchen dragging a trail of dirty slush behind me, my mind on one track only: water. I was filling a glass at the sink when somebody came up behind me and put his hands over my eyes. I figured it was Buck or Bill trying

107

to be cute, and I almost swung back before I decided I was too tired to start a fight. "Get off me, huh?" I growled, pulling away.

"Not until you guess who."

I started. "Kat," I said, taking her hands from my face and twisting around. "What the hell are you doing here?"

"Don't swear," she told me. She kissed me before going on. "I've been waiting for you for *hours...."*

"How long?"

"Since three."

I took time out to gulp my water. I was still thirsty after that, so I filled it up again and set it on the table before I slumped into a chair. Katy stood behind me and massaged my shoulders, which she knew I liked and which felt pretty good. I'd been all tensed up and hurting, but with her working on me the pain was going fast.

I closed my eyes and purred like a cat—which was a joke between us because I always called her "Kat." "The perfect little woman," I said a few minutes later, teasing. "Her joy in life is to wait for the man of the house to come through the front door so she can serve him—"

"Watch it," she warned.

"But, Kat, I'm proud of me. I'm training you good, huh?"

"You're going to get it in a minute," she said, digging her nails in my shoulders, which made me wince. "Besides, I wasn't exactly waiting for you in hopeful silence. I had Buck to keep me company."

Oh, man, the shoulders knotted right back up. It was involuntary, the way I reacted. I got up without looking at her and dumped what was left of my second glass of water in the sink.

Her lips pressed tight. "C'mon, Rich," she said,

talking down at me. "You aren't going to start that up, are you?"

I slammed the glass down a lot harder than I'd meant to. "Start what?" I demanded, annoyed to the point of anger.

"Oh, Rich." Her mouth twisted impatiently to the side and she talked to me like somebody talking to a child. "Don't play games. You know what."

"No, I don't know what or I wouldn't've asked." I turned my back to her and pretended to search the refrigerator.

Her foot tapped the floor. "I don't know what's wrong with you," she flung at me. "This isn't like you at—"

"*What's* not like me?" I said, vicious and short, cutting her off. Of course I knew what she meant, and I knew she knew I knew, but I wasn't about to give in on that point. The whole time a part of me was cringing with every stupid word. Katy and I weren't fighters and we were never petty like that. Red lights flashed and screamed at me to give the whole thing up, but I was too proud to give in. I was *somebody,* remember?

"It's not like you to be *suspicious,*" she said firmly. "Or *jealous.* Or *possessive.*"

I had an ugly sneer on my face. I can't believe Katy didn't just walk out the door. But she didn't, and I lashed out at her. "Who says I'm *suspicious?* Or *jealous?* Or *possessive?* Maybe you're just reading things into me that *should* be there."

"Oh, right!" she cried indignantly. "You don't care who I talk to. We trust each other, remember?" A flash of inspiration hit her, and her eyes flashed with it. "And you *don't* care, either, just like I don't care when you talk to other girls! It's Buck that bothers you, and I think that's pretty *sad,* Rich, pretty *sad.*"

I was furious with her like I'd never been before.

She'd hit the nail on the head, and I didn't want to admit she was right because it would mean admitting I was thinking things about my best friend and my girlfriend that I should never have been thinking.

For a minute I didn't dare say anything, because I had enough rationality left to know I would say something I'd be sorry for. I wanted to punch a wall in a bad way.

When I finally did talk, I said, "That's nowhere near true, and you know it."

She shook her head and stared at me, her look more pitying than anything else. "Then why are we fighting?"

I couldn't answer that. I slumped back into my seat and brooded.

"Today, Rich," started Katy very gently, "when you saw me and Buck after lunch . . . why were you so rude to him? You hurt him. You *know* we always walk together. But you had to make a scene out of it. 'Taking over my girl!' God! How would you like it if it was the other way around and he said that to you?"

I tried to remember what I'd said to them after lunch, but I couldn't. So I just denied it. "I didn't say that."

"You *did*. That's what you said. Sounds bad, doesn't it?"

I pressed the heels of my hands against my forehead. The anger and jealousy had all drained away, leaving me feeling as though I'd been reduced to nothing. "I didn't really say that," I said. I didn't even convince myself.

"You did."

"Oh, hell. . . ."

She came to me then, petting my hair like I was a little boy or a dog. "Just don't do it again,

Rich. Promise me that and I'll forgive you. But this has got to stop."

"I promise," I said humbly. She could have gotten me to promise her anything at the moment. I laid my head on the table. "I can't believe I said that...."

"You did," Katy told me again.

I was all right for a while after that fight, all right in the sense that I wasn't seeing things between Katy and Buck that weren't there. In other words, for a while after that fight I turned the other cheek, looked the other way. And turning the other cheek toward Katy and Buck—mostly Buck—forced my sight in some directions I hadn't turned to before. I started seeing some reality, a little more of what was going on.

Take what I happened to witness in the big garage behind the machine shop. I'd gone down there one day to find Mr. Hanson, the shop teacher, to give him a message from Mr. Flynn. There wasn't any class in the shop when I came in, so I worked my way to the back where his office was. That's when I heard Joe Parriot's voice, hard and rising.

"You little———" I heard him say. He used a whole string of four-letter nouns and adjectives I'm not going to write down.

I knew without a doubt that it was Parriot, even though the voice was coming through the walls from the garage. He had this rough distinctive voice and used this fake new York tough accent— fake, because he'd never set foot in New York a day in his life. I think he thought it was macho.

Anyway, I heard Parriot say that, and it didn't take half a second to come to the conclusion that something very wrong was going on.

Now, sure, curiosity killed the cat, but I wanted

to hear more. I wanted to know what was going on, and wanted to know with a weird driving passion. So I walked soft, real soft, to the door of the garage and stood just inside it. I couldn't see anybody at first, but then out of the corner of my eye I saw Parriot wave his illegal stiletto. He was against the left wall, almost hidden by a stack of boxes. I couldn't see anybody else.

"I'm only gonna say it one more time," said Joe, his voice a lot lower. He must've figured it wasn't a good idea to yell. "Now, I asked you nice. I asked you for a favor. But no, you can't *do* it. Well lemme tell you somethin'. Buck's gonna be real mad if you don't do like he asked me to tell you to do. Now I'm gonna ask you one more time...."

I should've listened to the rest, but I didn't. My mind was too busy reeling with everything that the mention of Buck's name could mean. What was he up to? Why was he recruiting Parriot to do dirty work? What *was* the dirty work? Why was Parriot pulling a knife over it? *What was going on?*

I didn't have much time to think about it. Parriot and a buddy of his were striding toward the door with these grim, satisfied looks on their faces. I moved back fast and slid into Hanson's office. Just as they came in through the door, the one I'd been standing in, I came out of the office as if I'd just gotten there and looked at them as though I'd just caught sight of them.

"Hey," I said carelessly. "You see Hanson anywhere around here?"

Joe and his buddy shot each other a look. The thought occurred to me that Joe might still be very resentful of the way I'd thrown him the night Tony got jumped. But Parriot only shrugged his thin, flannel-shirted shoulders and said, "Nope. He's upstairs somewhere."

112

I hung there a few long seconds. I would've given a lot to find out whom they'd been threatening. But they slouched there on the cement like they'd been planted there, and it was more than obvious that they didn't intend to leave and give me the chance to find out. I hung on a few seconds more, ignoring Joe's glazed but pointed stare. Finally, I asked, "Well, if you see him, uh . . . tell him Flynn's, uh, looking for him." I couldn't think of anything else to say and I wasn't getting any reaction, so I left.

The incident bothered me, really bothered me. Something told me I'd hit on something serious; like Tony and his painful inability to hold his own against Buck, there was nothing I could do about it.

It wouldn't leave my mind, that thing I'd overheard. All of a sudden I noticed things everywhere, things that were weird. And it was even weirder that I'd never noticed them before now.

I heard Buck's name everywhere I went. Class, cafeteria, home, halls, locker room. Buck Buck Buck, everywhere and anywhere. It was like my ear was tuned to his name and picked it out of any conversation within my hearing. What would Buck say, what would Buck do, who would Buck favor next, who would Buck look down on next, how would Buck react. Buck. Did the sun rise for Buck? I started to wonder, and I started to get a real paranoia concerning him.

And then there was Buck himself. He never noticed anything at all. He always looked grateful when he was paid attention to, and he was always nice and unprepossessing and golden. Except when something didn't go his way. The tawniness showed then, and that's when he'd let his teeth show. But those times were so smoothly covered

113

and he was so quiet and easy the rest of the time that nobody remembered or even noticed the times his teeth showed.

Questions grew in my mind, and I couldn't force them down anymore. I'd been able to force them down before. It was the bond between us that did that. But now—

Well, now there were questions. And they wouldn't go away.

Three days after the incident I'd overheard in the shop garage, I got up enough guts to ask Buck about it.

It came up abruptly. We were doing Thursday's dishes, all of them since breakfast—not by our own choice, I might add.

"Hey Buck," I said casually after what had been a long silence. "Just what is it you're getting into with Joe Parriot?"

He couldn't hide that the question had stung him. His mouth dropped a little. "What?"

"You heard me," I returned casually. It was a false casualness, and Buck took it as antagonism.

He looked at me. I could see the thoughts flicking past in those hooded golden brown eyes. "Yeah, I know I heard you," he said. "But I don't know what the hell you're talking about."

I chewed on that. I couldn't believe he was actually trying to deny it, work his way around it like that. That wasn't his way with me. I stared straight into him. "C'mon," I said. "Don't pull that with me. What're you getting into, Buck? I heard Parriot threatening some kid that you were 'gonna be real mad' if he didn't do what you told him to. Buck...I'm not going to say anything. Just tell me." Oh, righteous me.

He didn't seem to have heard. "When was this?" he demanded.

114

"Few days ago. Monday, around fourth period."

He drew himself in tighter and thought faster. I hadn't expected that. Don't ask me what I'd expected. Some kind of confession maybe, but not a tightening up. It cut me that he did that.

The hurt disappeared a few seconds later when he said, half thinking out loud, "I don't like that, what he did. Don't like it. He was using my name for something. I never told him to. I didn't ask him to threaten anybody. I wouldn't trust him to," he added, emphasizing the "trust" and pinning me with his expression.

So the hurt disappeared and guilt took its place. Buck had trusted me with things from his past that he couldn't trust anyone else with, and now I was throwing that trust in his face. I remembered Christmas, and how important it had been to him that he'd bought my watch with honest money. Why was I so quick to suspect the worst of him? Would I always be, knowing what I knew about him?

I saw all that, and I was sorry for it. More than a little crushed, I said, "It's just that I heard that . . . I thought it was—"

"You thought I was into McKinney's game."

That's what I'd thought, all right. I'd had nothing to go on but those few overheard sentences and made a heavy conclusion on them. Maybe the conclusion was dead wrong.

All I could do was shrug in agreement and admit, "Okay. So that's what I thought. You blame me?"

I may as well have slapped him in the face. His voice was tight and furious and hurt as he said, "Seems to me you been doing a lot of *thinking* lately. Just what do you think I am? Huh? I didn't get Joe or anyone else to threaten anybody for anything and I don't plan to, either. I don't have

115

to, dammit! Look, Rich!" My name was snarled. "I did what I did before because I had to! *Then* has nothing to do with *now,* and I hate it when you think it does! Really *hate* it!" He was almost savage now.

This was the second real fight we'd had. The first had been that night after I took Tony to the hospital. That split had never truly healed, but we'd both covered it up and gone our separate ways with it. This second fight really shook me, though. Buck had brought up the past and the past went deep. The past—his past and my knowledge of his secret—was what created the bond between us. But it was also what separated us, made us irreconcilably different.

The distance between us hurt, and the hurt made me mad. I wanted to get back, make him hurt too. "Hey, you listen, golden boy," I spat out, using the derogatory name Tony still used in reference to Buck. "You're too damn touchy! So I made a mistake! You think you're a special case just because you've been through a little. I got news. You're not. If you heard something like that about me, wouldn't you wonder? Wouldn't you wat to know what was going on? Or wouldn't you give a shit?"

He glared at me with hate in his eyes, which didn't intimidate me because at the moment I hated him too. It was so easy to hate him. It was as easy as liking him.

He took a step toward me, a threatening step. "Oh, what now?" I said corrosively. "Going to beat me up? Put me in my place like you did Tony? Don't you feel scared without a few friends to back you up?"

He trembled, he was so mad. "Don't throw that in my face!" he warned through clenched teeth. "None of that was my fault and you—"

"Bull," I interrupted. "You meant what you did to him."

He almost snapped then. Almost. Tears of fury ran down his face. "Don't ever say that again," he choked, "or you just might end up even worse than him, Rich."

That was worse than a direct kick to the crotch. It stunned me, left me cold as ice. Somehow I managed to throw back an empty, meaningless retort. "And you just got through telling me you didn't play McKinney's game...."

The hurt I'd felt before and was feeling now was reflected in his eyes. But they were masked with a cruelty that I'd never seen in him before. "I meant what I said," he told me, voice low and tight. "But I never said I didn't have games of my own...." A gasp or a sob came from him, and then he bolted.

I went blindly to the medicine cabinet and swallowed four aspirins to try to drown out the headache pounding in my skull.

Chapter 10

There was no forgetting or forgiving that second split. We didn't bother to talk to each other except when we had to, and it was amazingly easy for both of us to ignore any questions concerning what happened.

Some people at school sensed something was wrong, but nobody had any facts so there was nothing to feed the gossip mill. At home we just stayed out of each other's way, so there wasn't too much questioning there either, but I think Mom and Dad suspected. They tried to ask, but they were being evaded, and they knew it; they eventually gave it up and let us be.

It was bad. All the time there was that invisible wall hard and cold between us. Katy knew the most about it, and all I told her was, "We got in a fight." Buck may have told her a lot more—they talked a lot—but I don't think so. This was as personal to him as it was to me.

The wall between us aggravated another problem. With this new split between us, I had no desire to give him the benefit of the doubt, and my jealousy of him and Katy became an obsession with me, an ugly obsession.

I would wait for Katy at her locker only to have her come to it with Buck at her side, the two of them always close but never touching. That burned me. I didn't want him anywhere near her. And I hated myself even more for thinking like that. It went back and forth, back and forth, and it tore me up inside.

I'd catch them talking on the phone. Not often, but enough to make me snarl. Buck's name would fall so smooth and natural from Katy's mouth as she described some funny incident they'd gotten into together that I would want to bite her words off at the throat. It drove me crazy.

I tried to check myself, but the jealousy was just too much for me to keep down. At first I'd casually mention to Katy that I'd seen her and Buck together again—getting along well? She'd brush it off, and then I'd start to push.

"What're you around him so much for? What were you talking about? I want to know, Kat...."

And then sometimes I'd push too hard and she'd get mad. "You're cutting off my air," she'd throw at me. "I'm telling you, Rich, if you clamp too tight I'll have to fight you to breathe."

Then I'd get mad too and accuse her of imagining things and not caring that I cared and all kinds of related stuff.

Things were not going well for us, and most if it was my fault.

Still, no matter how rocky things were and how tense the relationship was becoming, nothing prepared me for what happened the weekend after Valentine's Day. Katy and I had exchanged tame cards—*tame* meaning that there was no intimacy, no specialness. But we went through it for the form of it, both of us, especially me, unwilling to admit the coolness. We had had something very good, and now it was fading.

I took her out to dinner and we had a nice time. No sparkle, no flash, but no fights, either. I took her home afterward, and even the kissing was pointless and shadowy, something that wasn't good anymore.

Even after all that, I still wasn't prepared.

Katy dropped in Saturday afternoon. One of her friends drove her over, and her visit was a surprise to me, not that I minded. Mom was volunteering somewhere, and Dad had dragged Bill off to an appointment with the orthodontist, and Buck had taken off somewhere. He'd asked if I wanted to come, but I hadn't felt up to spending hours in his company, so I said no. So it was just me and Christy and the dog and the cat at home when Katy knocked at the door.

After I let her in we sat in the kitchen awhile. Like always, the talk between us was comfortable and easy, but it had a new quality to it, a forced lightness. Here were two people making a nice polite effort to make conversation, but the two of them kept wandering off on opposite tangents only to clash or to forcibly pull the conversation back to a point. It was more difficult for Katy than it was for me. Something in me had turned off to anything that was a sign of wrongness. I rambled on and on and didn't pay any attention to the struggle on her face.

Finally, Katy put her hands flat down on the table—fingers tense like she was about to push herself away from it—and closed her eyes. She stayed like that for at least five minutes, I think, with me going on and on at some pretense of closeness, before she finally said, "Rich . . . *stop.*"

121

I stopped. "What's the matter?"

Her eyes, affectionate and pitying and tired all at the same time, focused on the top of the table between her hands. "Rich," she said. "This has got to stop."

It was the same thing she'd said when she asked me to stop seeing things between her and Buck. I was tense but casual and normal at the same time, knowing what was coming and desperately pretending I didn't. "What?"

"Us...just...us, Rich." Her sigh was long and shuddering.

"Kat," I said slowly. I felt a thousand years old. This wasn't happening.... "I don't know what you're saying." It was a bald lie.

"Us, Rich," she repeated. "We're not working anymore. Do you know what I'm saying? It's just not any good.... You know it isn't."

Deep, deep down I could feel the pain rise; even though I was succeeding at holding it down for now, I knew it would come up soon. "No," I told her, shaking my head. "That's not the way it is."

"I think it is," she said gently. I felt like she was years and years wiser. She knew what she was doing. I was being dumped. She wasn't hurting. She was a little sad, sure, but she was already over it in her mind. For me the pain was just starting. "I don't think we should see each other anymore."

"Why?" I said bitterly. Inside the frustrated sorrow heaved.

"We're not going anywhere anymore."

"Emotional bullshit." I couldn't stop myself from saying, "You're getting rid of me for Buck."

Her jaw tightened. "Even if it was Buck...which it isn't...would you rather hang on like this?"

I thought about that, really thought about it. "Yes," I said, and I meant it with everything I had. I would hang on to her forever if I could, even if there was nothing there holding us together.

She licked her lips. She hadn't expected that. But it didn't shake her from her path, either. She was determined and knew what she wanted to do. "I'm sorry you feel that way," she said a little too stiffly, a little too formally. "But it takes two. And I'm not willing to be tied up anymore."

Softly, I said, "Tied?"

"Sorry. Bad word. I meant...oh, I don't know what I meant, anyway. You get my point...."

"I get it." This isn't the first one you've lost, I reminded myself. You've got a lot of moving around to do. But somehow that just didn't help.

"We're still friends." It was a statement, not a question.

I nodded. Why not? We'd started that way and we'd end that way. Five years from now she'd be nothing more than a signature in my yearbook and the memory of a few good times.

But now was what counted. And now was hell.

Friends. That would never work. Not after what we'd been, what we'd done. Well, maybe. With a girl like Katy friendship just might be possible. With a girl like Katy...

"I need a ride home," she was saying.

"Huh?"

"I need a ride home."

"I don't have the car."

She studied me. "No problem. I'll call somebody."

"You could stay if you want." It was a blank statement. It had no meaning but the literal.

"No thanks," she said, getting up to pick up the kitchen extension. "I think it would be better to call."

Gravel crunched under tires in the driveway. Somebody was pulling in. It was Buck, back with the car. "There's the car," I told her in mid-dial. "I'll take you now."

She paused with her hand on the receiver. "You sure?"

"I'm sure."

Buck came in, bringing a blanket of icy air with him. There'd been no February false thaw yet. "What's up?" he said, spotting us in the kitchen.

I didn't say a word. I didn't trust myself to. Katy just gave a slight shake of her head. Buck stood there, the smile fading on his face but never quite leaving. "Something wrong?" he said finally, awkwardly. He looked like a pup with that stupid half-smile.

Katy said briskly, "We've decided it would be a good idea if we saw other people for a while." She was so sure about it. *We've* decided, she said. But it hadn't been we. It had been *her,* and I hadn't had the will to argue with her. And what a way to put it. *Saw other people for a while.* High school society would love it. The stamp of approval would be given right away. That kind of honest practicality I'd always admired in Katy now seemed disgusting. It made her plastic, emotionless.

Buck was obviously uncomfortable, and I was glad. I hoped he was thinking maybe it was his fault even if it wasn't. "Is there something I can do?" he said.

Yeah, I thought to myself. Go to Cuba. Leave me alone.

"Yeah," said Katy. "Could you take me home?"

This was *not* going to happen. I stood up. "I told you I'd take you ... Kat." I used my name for her deliberately, reminding her. Reminding her ...

She parried with a reply that was so modeled and perfect and social that I wanted to hit her. "Rich, we've broken off. Let's make the break clean, all right?"

Fine. She wanted Buck to take her home. That's the way it was and nothing I could do would change it. So I sat back down, facing away from both of them. "Go," I said. "Just go, then."

"Hey, Rich—" attempted Buck.

"*Go.*"

There were no more words. Just sounds. Buck jingling the keys in his hand, Katy sliding her coat over her shoulders, the front door opening and slamming shut. Crunching footsteps in the driveway, the metallic slam of two car doors. And then the roar of a warm engine fading down the street.

And after that there was nothing but the tinny noise from the TV in the den.

I didn't move after Buck and Katy left. I just sat there and let the hurt rise until finally I broke down enough to let myself cry.

The dog found me first. Captain padded into the kitchen, ears forward, nose questioning, and sat in front of me and whined and begged and nibbled my clothes. Usually, I don't pay much attention to him, but now I was kind of glad he'd noticed me. I slapped him around a little the way he liked, and the stupid animal was almost ecstatic that he'd managed to get me in a mood he understood.

Christy found me next. She wandered into the kitchen during a commercial in search of something to eat, I guess, but she forgot all about TV and whatever else when she saw me sitting there looking sick, which was how I felt.

"Where's Katy?" she asked, surprised, eyes wide.

"Gone," I said indifferently, like I didn't care. "Didn't you hear Buck come in? He took her home."

"I had my headphones on."

In spite of my misery, I couldn't help laughing. "Headphones while you were watching TV? Isn't that a little dumb?"

"I watched TV and listened to the radio," she said primly. Her eleven-year-old eyes searched my face. "Did you and Katy get into a fight again?"

I really didn't want to talk about it, but there was no reason not to answer her. "No," I told her. "We didn't fight. We broke up." *She* broke up, I told myself.

"Broke up" was a familiar phrase around the house. Christy was wise in the ways of "going together," if a little numbed to them from over-exposure. I thought she'd be satisfied with that and let it rest.

But she didn't. "Is she ever coming back?" she asked quietly.

I looked at her. Christy had really liked Katy. Katy had been a little bit of a big sister to her, and suddenly I hoped Katy wouldn't forget about her. It would hurt Christy to be forgotten like that.

"I don't know," I said. "I really don't...know...."

Christy didn't miss the catch in my voice. She came over and climbed into my lap. She was a little big for that kind of thing, but I appreciated it. "I'll be your girlfriend," she announced. "And I'll *never* break up with you, okay?"

The gesture was so sweet I almost broke again. Instead, I laughed a strained laugh and said, "Okay."

Christy could be an annoying smart-aleck brat, but she could also be a wonderful little kid, and at the moment I loved her more than anything.

I was upstairs listening to tapes when Buck got back. I was waiting for him, and when he finally made it upstairs I was ready.

126

"What took you so long?" I said acidly before he'd even come halfway into the room.

"What took me so long what?"

"What took you so long to get *home?*"

He kept his irritation under a lid, refusing to let me bother him. "I was cruising," he said.

"With Katy?"

"With Katy."

I hadn't expected him to answer so easily. And even though that was what I'd been thinking I hadn't wanted to hear it. Hearing it was like being punched. "Enjoy yourselves?" I said narrowly.

He looked at me, golden brown eyes hooded, animal. "She had some talking to do, Candy." Calling me "Candy" was his way of letting me know I was pushing it.

"Yeah, sure, sure," I said lightly. "Hey, she's a free woman now. Free for anybody who wants her.'

Irritation was transforming into anger and seeping out through the cracks. "Don't you talk that way about her. Breaking up is no reason to put her down."

I gave a short laugh. "I'm not putting her down. I'm stating fact. And even if I do put her down . . . so what? It's none of your business."

"She's a friend, and my friends are my business."

"Oh, and I'm no friend of yours, right?"

He whipped the keys he'd been holding at my head. The miss he made was intentional, but the thought behind the action was deliberate. "Why don't you shut up before you make a total ass of yourself?"

Oh, that made me mad. I wasn't going to back down now. I would blow up if it killed me. I grabbed those keys from where they'd dropped and held them between my fingers, silently begging him to give me a good reason to use them on his face.

127

"Yeah, yeah, step on me, golden boy, see what happens," I taunted, not caring what I said. "Was it nice having her, Buck? Isn't she good? Tell me something. Going to have her again, or throw her out like every other girl you use?"

He went white. He didn't dare come near me because he knew he'd get killed and that probably made him madder than anything. "You're messed up," he hissed. "I never touched her, and *I'm telling you Rich you better stop!*"

Oh, God, what was happening? A shudder went through me and I let the keys fall to the floor. The bond between us had become a chain, and all we were doing was cutting each other to pieces. And eventually one of us would bleed to death....

Whose fault was it? Not mine. I wasn't the one who was subverting everything. But I *was* the one who could stop it before it was too late.

And the fault wasn't all Buck's, either. He hadn't done anything wrong. His biggest crime was being in the right place at the wrong time. No. That wasn't right. There was something more....

"I'm sorry," I said. I didn't look at him. "I'm sorry."

Voice low, he said, "It's all right.... This is a bad day for both of us." It was a stupid flimsy excuse, but at least it was an excuse.

I held out my hand. "Friends?"

He hesitated for just a second before he took it. "Brothers," he said with a small smile.

It wasn't until hours later that it occurred to me to ask the question that had been nagging me since long before Katy and I broke up. I brought it up then because I thought I was over it, and I wanted to know. I brought it up out of the blue, leaning over the edge of the couch in the den to

What I didn't realize then is that all I'd do was push it way down deep where it bled with my even knowing it. I'd reverted to accep everything everybody told me without a figh cause to me that meant things were back t push him on the shoulder in the middle of some *Rocky* film.

He twisted up from the floor. "What?"

"Hey," I said. I had to know this and had to know it right then. "Were you telling the truth when you said you never...touched her? Katy?"

His shield went up fast. I couldn't read a thing. "Didn't you believe me?"

"Yeah, I believed you," I said hastily. "But I would've said the same thing if it'd been the other way around—even if it weren't true. I had those keys...."

He didn't say a word. He watched the movie.

"Look at me," I said, annoyed that he wouldn't answer. He did. "I don't care. All right? I don't care. I just have to know. Just for me. Understand? C'mon. I really don't care. Just tell me."

He glazed all over. That's the only way I can put it. He glazed. He was getting ready to lie and knew it.

"Tell me the truth," I said. "Please."

The glaze disappeared. He gnawed his lip. "Okay," he said finally. "We did. Nothing deep. Just friendly. Only once...and...today too. She's a good friend...."

There. I'd heard it and it had only made me bleed a little. I was over it already. "Thanks," I told him, and I meant it. He shrugged because he didn't know what else to do and went back to the movie.

mal. I'd gone back to not putting up a fight because leaving things the way they were was better. Easier.

I'd gone back to looking in the other direction.

thought you might want to, y'know? Ah, if you could just make it over here...."

Both Mom and Dad were home for a change, but Buck had taken the car, which left just the station wagon. "Hold on," I said.

I leapt down the stairs. "Hey Mom," I said, leaning over the rail to face the kitchen, "I need the wagon tonight, huh?"

Mom's voice floated through the wall. "It's supposed to be bad out later," she said, using the tone that meant no.

"I have to go," I said. "It's important."

"What is it?" she wanted to know.

"Homework," I lied. "Big project. I forgot about it...and I have to get some stuff from Tony Marinelli...."

"I wish you'd get this 'stuff' done on time," she started to lecture. But I yelled thanks in the middle of it and raced back upstairs. "I can make it," I said to Tony.

"Good," he said. He sounded relieved. "See ya in a few." He hung up before I could say anything more.

I pulled on my vars jacket and got the wagon keys for Mom and revved up the coughing engine. And then I drove fast, too fast, itching to find out what Tony Marinelli thought was so important that he had to have me at his place as soon as I could get myself there.

Tony had the door to his house open before I'd even pulled in along the side of the road. I locked all the doors—Tony lived on a bad street, a tough one—and cut through the soggy brown postage-stamp lawn, which was a mistake. I almost sank in it. Tony hauled me in the door and asked me if I wanted a beer.

I shrugged. "Why not?"

I followed him into the kitchen, taking off my jacket as I went. The kitchen wasn't exactly dirty, but there was a good-sized pile of dishes in the sink, and there were other signs all over the place that this was a house inhabited by men only. Tony's mother left him and his dad when Tony was around five and Mr. Marinelli had never re-married. Why bother when there were always plenty of women around to keep you company? Get tired of one, find another.

Tony snapped a beer out of a six-pack ring from a well-stocked refrigerator and flipped it to me and got another one for himself. It was a little different for me to be drinking on a weeknight without a party, but I took a seat and drank. After I'd started it occurred to me that I had to drive home, but I shrugged to myself and promised myself I'd take it easy.

Tony pulled out the chair opposite me and straddled it. For the first time I took a good look at him and noticed he wasn't exactly in the best of shape. He had on this grimy T-shirt he wouldn't have been caught dead in at school and also these beat-up old gray sweats that looked like they'd been through a war. His hair, which was always mirror-bound perfect during the day, was roughed up and sticking out like he'd been sleeping on it and hadn't bothered to comb it, and those big dark doe eyes of his had heavy circles under them.

It was weird to see him like that. Just a few hours ago in school he'd been the epitome of sharp-dressed jock. But now....Just let me say he matched his surroundings.

Don't get me wrong. He wasn't living in a way anywhere near cruddy. It was just looser, more run-down than I was used to, and the picture especially clashed because you'd think a guy like Tony would belong in rich wonderland. But he

Tony's eyebrows were raised, questioning. "He has a hold on a lot of people."

"I know that."

"He's not doing right."

"I know that."

"Tell me you think he's doing right."

"Marinelli, he's not doing right. I told you that."

"Then let's do something about it." He was intense and totally serious. He meant what he said.

All I could do was stare. Do something? What did he have in mind? Jump Buck like he'd been jumped? Did he actually think that would change anything? I shook my head.

"Forget it, Ton. Just forget it. You know how he is."

"Yeah, I know," he said grimly. "And I'm *tired* of it. I'm tired, man. I'm *tired* of being kicked around. I'm *tired* of him threatening me—"

"He threatens you?" I interrupted. No wonder he'd been so interested to know if Buck was on my case.

"Not personally."

"Buzz? Parriot?"

He nodded.

"Buck doesn't have anything to do with what Parriot does."

His mouth twisted. "You can believe that bull if you want but I know better."

"Dammit, Marinelli, Buck's a brother to me."

"Some brother. According to Parriot—who you can believe or not believe, man—if you'd made trouble with Katy, you would've got your ass kicked."

That stopped me cold. "If I'd made trouble—"

Tony nodded again. "That's how much Dawson thinks of her. He would've got you if you'd made trouble with him over her."

I couldn't believe it. I just couldn't. "You liar."

"I'm not lying about what I heard. Why would I?"

"Because you're so goddam jealous of him, Marinelli. And it shows right through the act you pull."

He wasn't mad at all—and that's what told me that my accusation was wrong. "Listen," he said. "Quit fooling yourself. He's doing right."

I was silent.

He hunched forward over the table. "You pick a side and you pick it now, Candy, before I say anything more. Either you crawl around nice and safe in Dawson's shadow and hope he doesn't accidentally step on you, or you can stop sticking up for him right now and start seeing what's going on and help point out to a lot of misguided believers that Buck Dawson does not walk on water."

All of a sudden I felt like nothing, dry and empty. Tony was making me choose. Choose between myself or Buck. Choosing myself was nothing more than backing Tony's revenge...or was it? What had Buck ever done for me? What did I have to show from him? Just a lot of pain, that's what. Nothing but a lot of pain.

I couldn't even say he was a friend anymore.

The last of my will to keep my head turned in the other direction peeled away. I saw everything dark in Buck. I looked at Tony across the table and my mind went back to how he looked on that night he'd been beaten up and how much I'd despised Buck for what he'd done and how he'd managed to convince me he was blameless and how Tony had moaned over and over, "I thought you guys were my friends." Tony and I went back a long time. Buck and I went back eight months. Flashes of Katy and Buck together spun in front of my eyes.

Damn the golden boy. Damn the stray with the

140

animal eyes. He'd used me. Damn Buck. Damn him.

I reached across the table to clasp Tony's hand in our old accomplice sign. "He's not going to threaten you again, Ton. And not me, either," I promised him. "Count on it."

He grinned. "We'll drown the water-walker."

I laughed, and it wasn't a pleasant sound. I was caught up in bitterness. "We don't have to drown him," I said. "He can drown all by himself."

That's when the light flared up from deep in Tony's eyes. "I've got something to show you," he said. "It's what I wanted you to come here for. Wait a minute."

He disappeared into the living room and came back with a rolled-up magazine in his hand. "Take a look at this," he said, spreading it out on the table.

I almost dropped dead. It was a porn magazine, a bona fide underground porn mag, the kind you have to go through a lot of trouble to buy. It wasn't the magazine itself that almost floored me, though—we'd gotten a lot of kicks going through Tony's dad's magazines when we were younger. It was the fact that this particular layout included Buck. There was no doubt in my mind that it was he. His hair was a little longer and bleached, but there was no mistaking those animal eyes. It was him, all right, caught in a bad way. I wondered if he'd known there were pictures. I don't think he did; he'd never told me about any.

"Who's that look like to you?" A note of triumph laced Tony's tone.

I got this sudden weird vision of Tony panting over a whole pile of those magazines and it kind of disgusted me. "I always hoped he was making it up," I said softly, more to myself than him. Much as I wanted to, I couldn't stop staring. I just couldn't believe it.

"Making what up?" Tony wanted to know. "What?"

"About what he'd done for a living back in L.A.," I said. And then it was like a dam breaking inside me. I came out with everything—everything—and didn't leave out a single detail of what I knew. It was a relief, in a way. It's hard to hold to a secret like that, because the harder you hold to it the harder it holds you.

Tony absorbed everything I said without a word. When I'd finished, he slapped me on the back and said, "Know something? You're right. He will drown himself. He will."

There was that sharpness in Tony, and suddenly I was uneasy. I shouldn't have said anything. I'd just willingly given Tony the power to destroy the closest friend I'd ever had.

Friend.

Was Buck a friend? I didn't know. I wasn't sure. But no matter what he was, I'd just broken a sacred trust. He'd trusted me with the deepest part of himself and I'd just thrown it away without even thinking. No, not without thinking. I'd known what I was doing when I told Tony about Buck's past. I'd wanted to hurt Buck, get back at him. But now I was scared, and guilty. I'd gone too far, and I was afraid that Tony would go even further. "Don't use this when you drown him. He's human, man. I don't want you hurting him that bad. Take him down but . . . don't . . . kill him."

"Hey, Candyman," said Tony, that old familiar arrogance flooding out. "You picked your side. Don't turn tail now."

"Don't you do anything you'll be sorry for."

Tony saw the look on my face and saw I meant it. I could actually see him thinking that I could let Buck know what was going on and he'd get killed. He drew closer. "Listen, Rich. I won't use this unless I have to. Just having it to hold over him should be enough to bring him down where he belongs...with the rest of us...."

"Keep in mind," I said, "how much it hurts you to get kicked in the teeth."

His eyes were dark and hard. "That's something you don't have to worry about me forgetting."

Chapter 12

I was pretty tense for a while after my talk with Tony, waiting for the ax to fall on Buck. Rumors, ugly rumors about Buck's past, began to circulate around school. I knew Marinelli was behind them. I don't know if Buck heard them, or if he did if he connected them to me. There was just enough truth in them that he could have, but we weren't speaking all that much anymore and I never found out.

But the rumors didn't bring Buck down. His position in high school society was too solid for him to be hurt by vague whisperings. If anything, his image was enhanced by the hints of something shocking and shameful in his past. So, pretty soon, the rumors died out and I began to relax.

That was a mistake. I should have known that Tony wouldn't be satisfied until he'd had his revenge. I should have known that he'd get impatient if something didn't happen soon. I should

145

have known that sooner or later he'd play his ace, in spite of his promise to me.

I got it all from Bob Cordero. He was there when it happened. He stayed away from it because it wasn't any of his business and he didn't want to make it his business but still he saw everything. He told me about it later because he figured I had a right to as much of an explanation as he could give me. Cordero was a good kid, a quiet one, and there's no doubt in my mind that what he told me was truth.

Buck's phys ed class was second period. Tony had some kind of half-semester elective, but he must've managed to get out of it for at least a few minutes. Because when the guys in the phys ed class came in from doing laps, that full-color spread Tony had shown me was taped across a couple of lockers.

Tony had played his ace.

According to Bob Cordero, Buck didn't even see it at first. The first thing he noticed was a bunch of guys all looking his way. Some just plain stared, some looked away, a few laughed—so Bob said— but the point is, Buck got the idea real quick that something was up. He ambled over, towel wrapped around his waist, water dripping down his shoulders, curious to find out what was causing the big stir. He still didn't have a hint of what it was all about. Cordero told me he would've given a lot to stop him from finding out, but at the moment he couldn't even look Buck in the face.

Of all the guys in the world who could've had their hands on that picture at the moment, it had to be crude-mouth no-tact total-jerk Kip Mason. Damn Kip for what he said, because what he said pointed all the blame my way.

The guys grouped around Kip kind of fell back when Buck strolled through, leaving Buck and

Kip to face each other. And Kip had to play his I'm-hot-and-tough game.

"So it's true, huh?" he said.

And Buck still didn't have a clue. "What?" he said evenly, smiling a little.

"What Marinelli said." Kip waved the magazine pages in front of his face. "About your mother and you pushing and all the rest—"

Buck pinned Kip's wrist with his right hand and grabbed the picture with his left and then he froze. "What Marinelli said..." His voice was a dry, rasping whisper. And then he stood there stricken, stricken and shaking. Cordero told me he never saw anyone with that hollow desperate look Buck had in his eyes, and I knew exactly what he meant.

Nobody knew how to react; nobody knew what to do, what to say. So they ignored him. It was quiet in the locker room then like it never was. Buck had moved into a corner by the time the bell rang, and when Bob left he was still standing there deep into himself, staring and trembling and crushing the picture in his fist.

Buck skipped his third-period math class—the class he had with Tony Marinelli. I know because that's when he came to the door of my computer class and told Mrs. Muller the office wanted me. The woman didn't think to ask to see some kind of slip. She just called for me to go to the office and didn't take a second look.

I got up and left, shutting the door behind me and almost tripping over Buck because he slouched right to the side of it. "Hey," I said, smiling, curious, "what're you doing?"

"I'm the office call," he said blankly, expression never changing. His face was empty, so empty I should've seen it for what it was right away and

147

been warned. And those eyes, those golden brown eyes . . . they were animal, more animal than they'd ever been before. More animal even than that first day I'd caught him in my car cringing like a trapped rabbit. . . .

He didn't say another word. He just turned and walked, which gave me a choice: follow and find out what he wanted or stand there like an idiot. So I followed.

We came to a set of stairs, the ones at the very end of the main building, the ones that led down to the basement. We went through those heavy steel doors and that's when he set on me. Right there in the nice soundproof stairwell.

His face wasn't empty anymore. He couldn't force the cover-up anymore. He was coldly furious, and the ice in his eyes made me back up a step. I opened my mouth, but before I had a chance to ask he spat out, "You *told*."

And I'd let myself believe that all the talk of his past that Tony had been spreading since that night when I'd spilled everything I knew about Buck had died. I'd stayed low and prayed my part in it would never come to light and hoped Tony wouldn't break his promise about going all the way with this. I'd thought it was over and done and I was safe. But I'd forgotten Marinelli's awful pride.

I'd done it, and Buck knew.

Despite all that, I tried to deny it. I guess it was only human to deny what I didn't want to be real, but the denial was so transparent it was pitiful. "Tell what?" I tried. "I didn't tell anything. . . ."

"Don't give me that shit!"

That hoarse whisper cut my words off in the throat. He was dead serious and he was hurting and he was going to make me hurt for making him hurt and there wasn't any doubt in my mind about what was coming. The best I could do would be to take everything without a word and tell him I was sorry after he'd taken it all out on me. Sorry ...as if that would be enough.

"You told," he repeated. "You told. You swore ...you know what you ...you knew that it ...it ... it *rips me apart Rich and you knew it would.*" He panted, chest heaving, breath rasping in his throat. He was caught between sobbing and snarling. Oh, the pain went so deep....

"I trusted you," he choked. He took a crumpled paper from a back pocket, unfolded it, smoothed it with a tense precision, held it out, and it was painfully familiar to me. There was nothing, nothing I could do or say to make things right. Nothing never nohow.

I couldn't look at the picture and I couldn't look at him. I kept my eyes on the floor. "I didn't have anything to do with that," I said in a low voice. "Tony found that himself, in one of his father's magazines."

He made a sound I think was supposed to be a laugh, a bitter, sarcastic laugh. "But you told..."

"It didn't make any difference. Tony would've—"

He grabbed my shirt and shoved me against the wall. I didn't make a move. I deserved what I got. I could rationalize all I wanted, but I had betrayed Buck's trust. I'd wanted to hurt him, to bring him down, when I did it. Just as much as Tony had.

"Don't give me that," he snarled. "Don't you give me that! You told, dammit, you told! You told *Marinelli!*"

He shoved me harder, like he wanted me to make the first real move. He wanted a real reason to kill me. "You told him," he said, "the only thing

149

I never wanted you to tell about.... You wanted to *get* me, didn't you...you hate me, you're so shitting jealous you wanted to *get* me...."

He went on and on like that, and those almost-truths ripped and ripped at me. It hurt like nothing else ever has. But still I didn't fight him because I'd done him a deep wrong and I deserved to hurt for it, hurt as much as he did now.

He crunched the paper in his fist and shoved that fist into my face. "You *eat* this for what you did." I guess he couldn't hold back the hurt and the fury anymore, because then he cracked my head against the wall and started to drag me down and pin me.

The pain was what fired me. Some kind of base survival instinct clicked in place. We fought each other like we were fighting for our lives, and in a way that's exactly what it was. It had been coming for a long time. Buck fought to keep the new life he thought he was losing and I fought to get back the old life I'd lost.

It was the most brutal fight I've ever been in. No holds barred. We aimed to damage. Anything we'd ever held inside before came out now.

It was a wonder nobody came along before they did. Even if we were out on the stairwell, we were far from quiet. Anybody going by would have seen or at least heard us. And people were always walking the halls. Still, it wasn't until we'd gone down half a flight of steps—Buck took a lot of damage there—that somebody heard or saw and ran for the teachers.

By the time the teachers showed, I was close to blacking out. I'd taken the worst of it by a mile. I had weight and height and expertise over Buck, but he had the will and the fury and that was everything. I didn't know then, but when he slammed my head against the wall he gave me a minor concussion along with a cut that had the back of my shirt soaked in blood. I broke my hand hitting him, and he messed up my face good.

He didn't have anything more than a lot of heavy bruises and a long, deep tear on his cheekbone that was probably from my class ring.

We were in the office before I could even stop breathing hard. They bawled us out and they went through all the phone calls and records and all that, but neither of us paid any attention to it.

Buck had lost his fury, and the only thing left was hurt. And he clamped down on that so tight that he may as well have been stone. I didn't like that look on him. Didn't like it at all. It wasn't normal.

There was a point while we sat there in the office that I came close to crying. Not because I hurt, which I did, but because of Buck's closing himself off. He was perfectly aware of what I was going through but he didn't move a muscle because he didn't care. He was past caring.

He was even past caring about himself.

Then we had to deal with the family.

After banning a wide-eyed questioning Christy and a strangely quiet, lip-chewing Bill from the kitchen, Mom and Dad sat Buck and me down at opposite ends of the table and then sat down themselves, hands tense on the edge of the table and faces creased with worry and sorrow.

They didn't know what to do, what to say, any more than me or anyone else. They knew next to nothing about the cause behind the splint on my hand and the bandage on Buck's face. We'd done such a thorough job of hiding our problems at home that my parents had hardly had any reason to even suspect conflict of this proportion between us. It was a shock to them. But still they tried,

tried their best to bring us out, build a bridge, find out what was wrong so they could help us help ourselves fix it. They tried, but the trying was really kind of pitiful, because they didn't know we were beyond a point where we could be helped.

"Why don't you tell us what happened?" Mom kept saying in one way or another. "We can't do anything for you if you don't tell us what happened."

Dad also tried . "You can't keep this between yourselves forever, boys. . . . It's got to come out sooner or later."

I didn't move, didn't meet anyone's eyes, and neither did Buck.

This went on for over an hour. My parents threatened and pleaded and reasoned, and none of it had any effect. We couldn't talk about it and that was that. Talking about it now would be nothing more than a lot of unnecessary humiliation for Buck—not to mention some hurting for me too—and I was at least that sensitive to him. I wouldn't spill anything, not anymore, anyway.

Once, though, after my dad said to Buck—or at Buck—"We've tried to be family to you, Buck. Don't you care about that at all? Doesn't it mean anything to you that we care?" Buck started to open his mouth, licked his lips a little. His mouth opened and a small sound, a sharp intake of breath, caught in his throat. For a minute his eyes pooled over, flooded with lost, hurt confusion. For just that moment he trembled on the brink of letting the dam break; but cruel and decisive as a steel trap, he snapped shut again and there was no more seeing inside him.

Finally, Mom and Dad said, "We'll talk about this in the morning. Maybe you'll have a different perspective after a night's sleep."

Quietly, Buck stood up and left the kitchen. As

soon as he was out of sight, my parents both pinned their eyes on me as if now that Buck was gone I would spout out everything they'd been trying to pick out of us in one neat little package. They looked at me and started with, "Rich—" But before they could say anything more, I just shook my head once, and they didn't say another word.

I eased my stiff body up out of the chair to get myself upstairs, and that was when Buck came stepping back down from up there, a blanket folded over his arm. My parents and I watched silently as he laid himself out on the couch in the den. Nobody said anything.

In a way that gesture of his hurt me more than anything else that had happened. It had a stark, simple finality to it that I couldn't stand. It almost brought me back to hating him; that's how much it racked me.

I went to sleep that night in a room I hadn't had to myself for a long time.

I started awake at three-fifty-nine A.M., so the display on the digital clock told. I don't wake up like that usually, so when I did then I was afraid, coldly afraid there in the dark because I knew the only reason I would've awakened was if something was wrong.

The first thing I did after lying there alert for a few seconds was go to the window and squint out at the dim street to see if something was the matter out there. The second thing I did was think of Buck and what had happened. Chills played down my back, and I didn't even have to spring down the stairs to check the den to know he was gone.

I just knew with dead certainty that he was... gone. He was a runner and he was gone for good. And somehow, the same something that told me he was gone told me it couldn't have been any other way.

I flicked a switch in the den, shading my eyes against the sudden flood of brightness, half-waiting for Buck to pop up from behind the couch or something, laughing at his joke. But there was nothing there in that ghostly empty den, nothing except a neatly folded blanket at the foot of the couch.

I took a deep shuddering breath and closed my eyes and listened to the silence.

I didn't go to school the next day. I didn't even think about school, and for the first time in my memory, neither did my parents. We were too busy attempting to cope with the gaping hole Buck had made in our lives to deal with something as trivial as school. This was a family crisis, and the family was together for it.

The day after that, though, I did go to school. The police had been called; I'd been raked for every detail I could safely give up; we'd had all our family conferences and made all the decisions and conclusions we could for now. I wasn't doing anybody any good sitting at home.

School was chaos. I was almost torn to pieces—figuratively—by people wanting to know more, more, and more details about this wonderfully exciting fight between Buck and me. This was the best piece of gossip to hit the fan in a long time. Not since Tony had been beaten up had the gossip lines hummed so hot and heavy.

I didn't tell anybody anything. I just wasn't up to it yet. Nobody knew Buck had gone for good, and I kept it to myself, a dark ugly secret, at least for a while.

Sixth-period study hall was a perfect reflection of the state of the whole school. When I came in

Tony was already there, and he radiated newly regained power. He was smug and cocky and confident, and the social stratum in the room was uncertain, hesitant. Until this week it had been mixed, with burnouts sitting with jocks, and jocks in back with burnouts, and socials giggling indiscriminately at them all. And it had been a fairly comfortable thing. But Tony had stepped in and reasserted himself, and he was throwing a very cold shoulder toward anything that didn't conform with the old clique codes—his codes.

I came in the room, and when Tony turned and flashed an even white canine grin at me and said, "Hey, Candy, c'mere! Wha'sup?" I wanted to be sick right then and there. But I just silently went over and sat down and bided my time, my thoughts at a slow boil all the while.

The bell rang, and the seating arrangement ended up loose, mixed, but Tony was a nucleus in a definite circle of jocks. At the moment he was in, a source of gossip and speculation. He was the one who'd discovered Buck's past, and the crowd wanted to be in on it.

I wanted to talk to Tony. I wanted to dissect him, and I wanted it badly. He knew it, too, knew it full well beneath that casual boisterous buddy stuff he fed me and everyone else, and it showed in the way he sometimes paused and caught his tongue in his teeth mid-sentence when he attempted some especially bad line on me.

"Marinelli," I said suddenly, darkly, hunching over my desk, "I'm going to throw up."

That startled him. For a moment his dark heavy eyes lost their mask and he was open. "Huh?"

"I'm going to throw up," I repeated decisively. I looked sideways at him. "I need you to take me to the nurse's office—now."

"Candy—"

"Now!"

Embarrassed, at a loss, he reluctantly swung his leg over the bar on the right side of his desk to grab my elbow and haul me up, avoiding the curious stares of everyone around us by looking at the floor. I let him drag me up to the desk where old Mrs. Weber stared owl-eyed at us from behind an attendance book.

"Uh...he's sick," Tony mumbled.

Mrs. Weber peered at us. "What's that?"

Tony shifted. I tried to look pale. "He's sick," he said again. "He's going to, uh, throw up."

Mrs. Weber visibly drew back. "Oh!"

"He needs to go to the nurse...."

"Certainly...certainly," said Mrs. Weber quickly, waving a birdlike hand at us. "Go right ahead."

Tony's fingers dug into my arm as he pulled me out the door and down the hall. After a few yards I hung back, yanking away from him. I stood stock-still against a locker, looking at him.

He looked back. "Don't you gotta throw up?"

I would've laughed if I hadn't been so seriously ready to give him hell. He'd really thought I was sick. Oh, God. "No," I said shortly. "Marinelli... Buck's gone."

I watched as first confusion, then comprehension, dawned on him. Emotions struggled for dominance on his face; he didn't know how he should react.

"That's what you wanted, isn't it?" I said softly. "To get Buck out of your life for good? Well, you did it, didn't you? Proud of yourself, Marinelli?"

His head snapped up. His eyes were troubled. "I didn't make him go."

I did laugh then. It was a laugh devoid of any kind of feeling. "Yes you did, and you know it. What you did made him run. Hope you feel good

156

about it, Marinelli, for driving him right back to where he came from."

He pivoted sharp on his heel, folding his arms tight against his chest and turning his shoulder to me. "I don't need this from you." The words were strangely empty of any sign of temper. They were flat, bare.

"Nobody needs anything," I countered. I tapped the bone in his elbow with the cast on my broken hand. "I didn't need this. I didn't need you using me like you did. Buck didn't need you totally destroying what little bit of a chance he had with that picture in the locker room...."

Voice low, hugging himself tight, he said, still half turned way. "I didn't need three of my best buddies smashing up my ribs.... What do you think that felt like, huh? Seeing your buddies trying to kill you, really honest-to-God kill you...." His voice shook.

"I know what it felt like!" A deep pang cut at me. I did know, I really did, and I was forced to emphasize. "What do you think happened with me and Buck? Huh? You're a loser, Marinelli! I'm giving you my problems face-to-face, not going around kicking your feet out from under you from behind your back. And you know I could do it, too," I said emphatically, harshly. "I could, Marinelli, I really could. People loved Buck...." I paused, took a deep breath. "This school doesn't need you. It spit you out once and it'll happen again. Soon as all the novelty wears off and people know Buck's gone and what's behind it and who's behind the what. ... Well, you'll be nothing then. Big fat nothing. And I'm the one who knows the whole story.... I could break up what you think you've got back for yourself so easy it's not funny."

He'd turned back to me by now, turned back and stared open mouthed. He knew what I said was truth, and for the first time in a long time I saw him scared. He knew he had no way out from this and he didn't even have the consolation of putting me in the wrong because he knew I was right. "Rich," he said uneasily, forgetting to be a jock and use my last name, "c'mon..."

"You'd deserve it, too, for what you did," I said, relentless. "God...for a little bit of petty glory you messed up a guy for life.... For *life!*"

"Rich...I'm sorry." He looked straight into me. All of a sudden, like that night I'd gone to his house after he'd called, I was plunged into the past, a past when there'd been no Buck and when people seeing us play catch in the street as kids had thought we were brothers or something because we had the same thick dark hair and—at the time—similar faces and builds. I didn't want to think about the past, but it was there and I did.

"I'm sorry," he said again. "You do whatever you want to do...I can't stop you. But you'd be just as guilty as me or...Buck, if you did, and you wouldn't have anything over on either of us then."

Suddenly I was tired of all of this. "Oh, shit, Ton," I sighed. "I'm sick of having anything over anybody. I'm sick of fighting and getting back at people. Let's just stop all of this crap."

Tony relaxed a little then. "Friends?" he asked almost plaintively.

I smiled just a little. "You watch yourself, Ton. Don't you use people."

"Hey, Candy...."

I tried to lighten things up a little. "Oh, c'mon, wha' do'you want now?" I said, grinning to show I was kidding.

He was somber. "You really think I—You really think Buck...uh...went back?"

That was like cold water down my neck. My

grin disappeared. "I don't know," I said slowly. "I really don't know."

"Would you believe me if I said I hope he didn't. . . . y'know?"

"Yeah," I said softly. "'Cause I hope so too."

Chapter 13

It was about a week after Buck left, during first period, when Katy passed me a folded scrap of notepaper. It read, *I need to talk to you.*

I looked at her. We still sat next to each other, but since we'd broken up we hardly spoke at all. There was that wall between us, a wall that didn't allow for much discussion. But she'd passed me that note, and I wondered.

She was busy with homework, but I knew she knew I was watching. She also knew that I knew exactly what she referred to in that note; what it referred to made my mouth dry. She wanted to talk about Buck, and this was something I did not do. At home the subject was still painful, hurting; my parents were spending a lot of time and money trying to get a lead on Buck and it was a constant effort for me to keep from being overwhelmed by the emptiness inside me. At school the whole story from beginning to end was twisted, glamorized, mangled beyond any kind of truth, and I shied away from my part in it. People learned quickly that I turned off any personal questions.

But Katy was the one person who could say she needed to talk to me about "it" and really mean it. It wasn't gossip she was looking for, but understanding. And I wanted her to understand. I wanted her to know my part of it all from my own mouth.

So I scribbled, best as I could with my left hand, *When?* and tossed it onto her open book. She opened it, wrote something, tossed it back. I read, *I have a pass to get you out of second period if you want to. I'll wait for you in the auditorium.* Even as I read it she handed over a near-illegible pass that said *Yearbook Photography* and bore the signature of some teacher whose name I couldn't make out.

Out loud I said, "Okay."

When I showed up, she was there waiting, perched on the edge of the empty stage, feet dangling over darkened lights, books piled beside her.

"Hi," I said. My voice seemed dry and flat, swallowed up by the huge dusty space around us.

"Hi," she said. Her voice was swallowed up too.

I walked out to front center stage, looking out over rows and rows and rows of hard empty symmetrical seats. "Why here?" I asked, staring up into the dim shadows of the balcony.

"No one else is here right now."

"Oh." I dropped myself down on the edge of the stage, a few feet away from her. I studied my beat-up old high-tops as I kicked the concrete base of the stage with a heel. "What did you want to talk about?"

Her eyes lowered so that her lashes touched her cheek. "You know."

"It's a pretty wide topic of conversation."

162

"Tell me what Buck ever did to you to make you do what you did to him."

I stopped kicking. Those words were the last I'd expected from her, and they hurt, really hurt. Staring, I said, "What do you mean, what did he ever do to me? Lord, Katy, it wasn't what he did to me. It was what he did to everyone...to the school!"

Her look was sharp. Dryly she said, "I hadn't noticed anything particularly horrible."

"Kat—" The old nickname slipped out. I licked my lips. "You can't tell me you didn't see it."

"See what?"

"What he did! He controlled this place...and he used anybody he could to do it. Listen. You remember when Tony got beat up? Do you? Well, that was Buck's fault. Buck made that happen! I was there. I saw it.... Think I'd lie about it? C'mon, don't look at me like that! There's still blood on the backseat of my car from when I drove him to the hospital...."

She looked away. "A lot of people said Tony deserved it." She said it like a challenge.

"Nobody deserved what he got. Nobody."

"It doesn't justify what you did to Buck."

"Look, I didn't—" I cut myself off. I'd snarled like a teased junkyard dog. "Look," I started again, a lot more softly, "if you're just here to cut me up, then don't bother. I don't need it. You think I'm all peachy overjoyed with everything that happened? You think I *like* sitting around my house every night wondering where he's at and what he's doing?" I was so worked up with it that my throat constricted on me. I had to force the words out. "I feel like dirt, okay? Is that what you want from me? A confession? Well, there it is. You got it. I feel like *dirt*."

Silence spread between us. It felt like an hour,

but it was only a minute or two before Katy said, "I didn't mean to accuse you like that."

"Yeah. It only sounded that way."

"Rich—"

"Sorry."

"It's just that—"

"What?"

"I . . . wish he hadn't gone."

That got me. "Did you like Buck that much? Really like him?"

"That doesn't have anything to do with it. And even if it did," she added fast, too fast, "that would only make me feel worse about it all."

A retort sprang up in my mouth. But we'd been hitting at each for ten minutes straight now. I just didn't feel like keeping it up anymore. I wanted her with me, not against me. "If it helps you any . . . I wish he hadn't gone, too. Believe me, that's the last thing I wanted for him."

"What did *he* want for him?"

"I wish I knew."

Her fingers drummed the stage. "He wasn't bad. Not bad bad. Not underneath. If he was bad to people . . . it was just a show he put on, to protect himself or something. He could get hurt so easy. . . ."

"Maybe."

"What do you mean, maybe? Rich, he was your brother! Even if it was just for a while. . . . You can't tell me you two hated each other every minute. I know you didn't! Buck thought so much of you."

"You've got to admit he had a weird way of showing it."

"Maybe he showed it the only way he knew how."

"You think that never occurred to me?"

"I don't know what to think. You're so . . . well . . . harsh, with the way you talk about him and all these things he did. What else am I supposed to think except something really awful happened between you two?"

"Something awful did happen," I said slowly. "He got scared. He and I were close like he'd never been close to anyone his whole life and that got him cold. He thought being close like that was just asking for someone to take advantage of you...."

"So he took advantage of you first," she said.

My eyes snapped to meet hers. "Yeah. Yeah, he did." I looked down then. "I guess that's why I'm harsh...because I'd rather have it be all his fault, you know? I mean, I did exactly what he was most scared of in the end. I broke his trust."

"Sometimes," she said, voice so low it was hardly more than a whisper, "when people are really hurting, they don't think."

"Kat...what're you saying?"

"I'm saying you...you and Buck both...you were hurting. And neither of you did a lot of thinking."

I wanted in a bad way to put an arm over her shoulders, to have her hug me quick and laughing like she used to. But I didn't even think about trying, except in the very back of my mind. It wasn't the time or the place, and I was too washed out. Too washed out with thinking about it all.

"Rich...do you think he'll come back...after he thinks a little?"

The question gripped me. I'd never considered the possibility, not really. His leaving had hit with a hard finality that didn't allow for thoughts of him ever returning. Would he come back? I didn't think so. No. Not after what had happened, not after that betrayal he knew way deep down he as good as asked for. He would move on, look for a new way to forget, to survive, to make it. "He's a runner," I said to her, and that's all I said. There was nothing more than that to say.

"What if he did come back? What would you do?"

"I'd say, 'Welcome back.'"

"Rich..."

"Hmm?"

"You did Buck a lot of good. More than anyone else, I think. You shouldn't blame yourself."

That touched me deep. Quickly, lightly, to cover up, I said, "Oh, I never did."

"Maybe he'll come through okay."

"Hope so." My heart beat fast.

"Bell's going to ring any minute." She was toying with her watch.

I flicked a glance at my wrist. She was right; we only had a couple of minutes left in the period.

Then I looked at my wrist again.

The watch, the gold watch Buck had given me way back in December on Christmas Eve that seemed like it was years and years in the past rather than just a few months ago, was what I used so casually just now to check the time. I'd never really paid attention to it until now, had never thought of it as a piece of himself that Buck had left behind. I put it on every morning, wore it all day, and took it off at night. It was a good watch, but wearing it was nothing more than a habit.

Looking at it now, though, brought up a rushing mixed-up flood of thoughts and memories.

I remembered how shocked I'd been when I opened up the box he'd practically thrown at me and saw that watch there...and I remembered how even then I couldn't stop suspicion from floating around, when I asked him how he got the money to pay for it.

Oh, yeah, we'd had our close times, times when

he was as shining and golden as the watch. That was where his charm came from, all that charismatic vulnerable golden charm that drew people to him like iron filings to a magnet. It came from the glittery side of him, the needing side. The side that trusted me.

But then there was his other side. The ugly side, the manipulative side, the driven side. The side he let control him.

The side I'd reacted to when I broke his trust.

I didn't understand that side of him then. I didn't understand it now, either. How could I? I'd never lived like he had, never had to claw around in dirt to stay alive. He'd been taught the hard way from the day he was born that you had to be in control to get where you wanted and that survival and being on top were the only things that mattered. He went the only way he knew when he took Tony down and made connections with Buzz. He just didn't know anything different. Fear of hurting drove him, and hardened him.

That was Buck's mistake. He figured that the only way he could avoid hurting and get where he wanted to be was by keeping people out, by manipulating. What he didn't realize—or never learned to care about—was that he hurt people by this. Hurt them enough to make them want to lash back at him.

There was no doubt that there was good in Buck, though. There was a lot of good; the watch was proof of that. He just didn't let it come out. As I kept studying the watch, flexing my wrist and watching the light play over it, I wondered what kind of person Buck might have been if his life had been different.

But that kind of wondering was pointless. All I could hope for now was that Buck would remember the good, remember that he'd been happy, really happy, for the first time in his life because he'd tried to open up for a while and trust people. I hoped, too, that he'd understand that it was his own hardness that drove me to break his trust. The day he understood that—the day he let the golden side carry him rather than the hard side—would be the day he'd start his way back to the home he'd had with me and my family. Or maybe that would be the day he'd make a home for himself.

I prayed it would happen soon. I was scared for him. He could break if much more happened to him.

I put my arm behind me and looked at Katy. "Did I tell you everything you wanted to know?"

"I think you did," she said.

"Kat..."

"What?"

"Never mind."

Like she predicted, the bell rang, clanging furiously just above our heads and echoing around in the halls. We both jumped.

"Are you sure?" she said when the bell stopped. She gathered up her books and stood to leave.

"Yeah."

Hesitantly, like she was afraid of saying something wrong, she said, "Thanks for talking to me."

"Yeah." She didn't need to thank me for that.

She looked at me for a few seconds longer, blue eyes big as she paused before the double doors at the side of the stage, and then she turned and left. I didn't move.

I sat there lost in my thoughts alone in that dark old auditorium until the bell rang again five minutes later for third period. And then I sat there some more.

TAMELA LARIMER was seventeen when she wrote BUCK, which was selected from 400 submissions as winner of the 1985 Avon Flare Young Adult Novel Competition. She also has received Honorable Mention from *Scholastic* for two of her short stories. Currently a student at Pennsylvania State University, where she is majoring in English, Tamela Larimer hopes to become a full-time writer.

ATTENTION TEENAGE WRITERS!

You can win a $2,500 book contract and have your novel published as the winner of the 198 Avon Flare Young Adult Novel Competition

Here are the submission requirements:

We will accept completed manuscripts from authors between the ages of thirteen and eighteen from January 1, 1989 through August 31, 1989 at the following address:

The Editors, Avon Flare Novel Competition
Avon Books, Room 818, 105 Madison Avenue
New York, New York 10016

Each manuscript should be approximately 125 to 200 pages, or about 30,000 to 50,000 words (based on 250 words per page).

All manuscripts must be typed, double-spaced, on a single side of the page only.

Along with your manuscript, please enclose a letter that includes a short description of your novel, your name, address, telephone number, and your age.

You are eligible to submit a manuscript if you will be no younger than thirteen and no older than eighteen years of age as of December 31, 1988. Enclose a self-addressed, stamped envelope for the return of your manuscript, and a self-addressed stamped postcard so that we can let you know we have received your submission.

PLEASE BE SURE TO RETAIN A COPY OF YOUR MANUSCRIPT. WE CANNOT BE RESPONSIBLE FOR MANUSCRIPTS.

The Prize: If you win this competition your novel will be published by Avon Flare for an advance of $2,500.00 against royalties. A parent or guardian's signature (consent) will be required on your publishing contract.

We reserve the right to use the winning author's name and photograph for advertising, promotion, and publicity.

If you wish to be notified of the winner, please enclose a self-addressed, stamped postcard for this purpose. Notification will also be made to major media.

Waiting Time: We will try to review your manuscript within three months. However, it is possible that we will hold your manuscript as long as a year, or until the winner is announced.

VOID WHERE PROHIBITED BY LAW.

6.35